D0933612

BOOKS BY ROGER L. SIMON

Heir
The Mama Tass Manifesto

THE MOSES WINE DETECTIVE NOVELS

The Big Fix
Wild Turkey
Peking Duck
California Roll
The Straight Man

THE STRAIGHT MAN

VILLARD BOOKS
NEW YORK
1986

STRAIGHT

MAN

A
MOSES
WINE
DETECTIVE
NOVEL

ROGER L. SIMON

Copyright © 1986 by Roger Simon

All rights reserved under International and Pan-American Copyright Conventions. Published in the United States by Villard Books, a division of Random House, Inc., New York, and simultaneously in Canada by Random House of Canada Limited, Toronto.

Library of Congress Cataloging in Publication Data
Simon, Roger Lichtenberg.
   The straight man.
   I. Title.
PS3569.I485S7   1986   813'.54   86-40105
ISBN 0-394-55837-5

Manufactured in the United States of America

9 8 7 6 5 4 3 2

First Edition

Book Design: Jessica Shatan

FOR RAPHAEL AND JESSE

WHEN THE ANALYSIS IS OVER,
THE PROBLEMS BEGIN.

—SIGMUND FREUD

THE STRAIGHT MAN

1 There's nothing like a shrink for making you feel depressed. Five months ago, when I walked into Dr. Eugene Nathanson's office, wondering what to do with my life, I wasn't feeling *that* bad. And it wasn't just that he was a shrink. He was a cripple. Sitting there in a wheelchair, for crissakes. Here I was with my little problems and this guy had had poliomyelitis or something at the age of six or whatever and still was a full-fledged psychiatrist with a thriving practice in Santa Monica Canyon.

He smiled at me politely as I sat in a beige leather Eames chair angled between his desk and a photograph of an aging Jewish bohemian I later learned was Fritz Perls, the founding father of Gestalt therapy.

"What can I do to help you?" he asked, pressing a servo-control that straightened the motorized back of his wheelchair.

"I'm not exactly sure." I hesitated, looking at Nathanson. He was a dark man with thick eyebrows, and the dim lighting in the room gave him an ominous, almost menacing cast. "I just quit a job as security director of a computer company and I don't know what to do next."

"What would you like to do?"

"Maybe expand. Start my own detective agency. But . . ." I shrugged.

"You are a detective . . . ?"

"A private detective, yes."

He didn't react, although I assumed he didn't have a lot of PIs wandering into his office. At his location he was more likely to get lawyers' wives and frustrated screenwriters.

We sat there awhile not saying anything. At that moment my problem seemed increasingly mundane, almost dumb. I had come to a psychiatrist for career guidance? At ninety-five bucks an hour, that was pretty stiff, considering you could get much the same thing from one of the brighter clerks in the back cubicles of the unemployment office.

"You seem depressed." He spoke as if this were simply a fact. Nothing more.

"I guess I am," I answered, looking away uncomfortably past his wall of books to a cactus outside his window.

"How do you experience it?"

"What do you mean?"

"How do you *feel* it . . . in your body?"

"Well, uh, it's a kind of ache . . . in my stomach . . . near the groin."

"Describe it to me more precisely."

And that was the last I heard of my career problems for a while. I spent the next few weeks playing Gestalt games—rolling around on the floor, going from chair to chair inventing crazy conversations with my parents and children, yelling at old girl friends and my ex-wife, jumping up and down like an Indian in a shamanistic trance and generally acting like some kind of lunatic on a drug-free acid trip.

"So what does this all have to do with why I can't get it together as a detective?" I finally asked him after another session of standing on a desk proclaiming like Cicero in front of the Roman Forum.

"What do you think?"

"What do *I* think? ... What do you mean, what do I think?" I got angry whenever he got conventionally shrink-like on me, refusing to answer my questions directly. "Look," I said. "It's my dime here. I'm the client and we're on a fee-for-service basis. If you think you know, tell me."

"Okay, you want a clinical diagnosis? You're suffering from a dysthymic depression caused by acute diminution of self-worth probably stemming from trauma during the oral phase of child development. Now, does that help you?"

"Not a whole hell of a lot."

"I didn't think it would."

"How about I'm feeling lousy because I had a high-powered job and I'm back to being a gumshoe again?"

"That makes sense."

"So what does that mean, Dr. Shrink? Every time I have some kind of reversal I'm going to plunge into depression?"

"Until you learn how to do something about it for yourself."

"How do I do that?"

"Find out why you don't. Find out what you get out of failing."

"Find out what I get out of failing? An empty bank account—that's what I get out of failing. If it hadn't been for my fancy computer job, I couldn't even be here paying you."

But that, obviously, wasn't all of it. I got a hell of a lot more than that out of failing, and in the weeks to come, I found out more about it than I wanted to know.

"So your initial sense of failure came from your father ..." Nathanson prodded me slightly one afternoon further along in the therapy.

A sudden sadness came over me as I remembered my father, who had died several months before. He had been a successful corporate lawyer with a powerful Wall Street firm who often disapproved of what I did, although he didn't say it. I had strong feelings of loss now that he was gone, but also a nagging discontent, as if there were something unfinished between us. Maybe it was because I never completed law school.

Nathanson must have noticed this, because he said, "You know, Moses, it's not just grief. Most patients seeking psychotherapy suffer from disturbances of self-esteem like yours ... feelings of inner emptiness, lack of initiative ... social or sexual maladjustments of various kinds ... usually stemming from some problem in their relationships with their parents. But"—he stared directly at me—"I have confidence that with time you're going to work yours out."

At that particular point in time, I didn't share his confidence. I had gone back to my private investigative practice in Los Angeles with all the enthusiasm of a clerk at the Motor Vehicles Bureau. Process serving, missing persons, insurance claims—I moved from one to the next like an automaton. Even an ecology-oriented case involving a massive toxic waste suit in the Valley scarcely interested me. My social life was, as that kid wrote, less than zero. And with the AIDS scare, like everybody else with half a brain, I was

watching my random contacts, even though they were het-
erosexual. Even my fantasy life wasn't much. My only
concessions to personal pleasure were the turbo-charged
BMW I had left over from my high-paying job at Tulip Computers and the overpriced, undersized *moderne* apartment I
rented on Kings Road in West Hollywood with a panoramic
view of the city and a useless wet bar.

My visits to Nathanson had become the true focus of my
life. Three times a week I would troop into his office. Meanwhile, I would spend sleepless nights, dousing myself with
Dalmane and sinsemilla to get two hours of fitful rest before
I had to meet another depressive dawn.

During that insomnia, I was prey to vicious night
thoughts. My children were growing up and leaving me.
All my relationships with women ended in disaster or ab-
surdity. My friends were deserting me—or were bored with
me. I was a fraud in work, a second-rate gumshoe who had
never finished law school. I had nothing to look forward
to but forty more years of repetitive depression. The truth
was obvious: from here on in, I was on a straight-line path
to Skid Row.

"It usually gets worse before it gets better," said Nathanson, one session after he returned from a brief vacation in
Maui.

"Thanks. It gets any worse and you might as well put me
on intravenous morphine."

"An interesting case might help you."

"I thought an interesting case was merely a temporary
distraction from my problems ... that I had to find tranquillity in myself."

Nathanson smiled. "You really are hard on yourself, aren't you?"

"Brutal."

"Did you ever think maybe you expect more of life than most people?"

"That's not a very shrinklike thing to say. I thought I was paying you so I could have it all."

This time Nathanson didn't smile. He pressed his servo to right himself the way he did at the end of a session and stared directly at me. I was aware once again of his thick eyebrows, his dark, almost black eyes that were at once penetrating and menacing.

"Moses, this is one of the more unprofessional things I've ever done—perhaps it's even a first—but a client of mine is in great need of help. Your kind of help."

Immediately I felt a strange discomfort. Under normal circumstances I would have been perfectly delighted to get new work, especially work that promised to be interesting. But here? This was my safe haven from the world's distresses—untouched by women, work, parents, children. Even my own loneliness. Everything could be safely "reexperienced" and "integrated." I could become whole again. But . . . at the expense of a job?

"I see you're concerned about something, Moses. What is it?"

"I don't want anything interrupting the work here."

"Do you think it would?"

"I don't think I'm finished."

"Yes, I agree with that. You're making some progress, but—"

"*Some* progress?"

"Yes. Some. You have had certain therapeutic resis-
tances, like any patient. Look—" He spun his wheelchair
toward me about half a foot. I always marveled at his dexterity. "I promise to redouble my efforts on your behalf. I
owe you at least that much if you do this for me. I'd be very
grateful, Moses, and so would my client. And feel free to
charge her any fee you feel would be fair. She can afford
it."

"Who is she?"

"Emily Ptak."

"Emily Ptak . . . not Mike Ptak's wife?"

"You know her?"

"No, but I certainly know who *he* is—or was. Otis King's
straight man."

I didn't have to elaborate. It was clear that I knew what
everybody else in L.A. did. And half the rest of the country
as well. One week before, Mike Ptak, a former late-night TV
comedy star, had taken a fifteen-story dive off the penthouse
of the Albergo Picasso hotel on the Sunset Strip. He had
landed in the valet parking area of the Fun Zone—America's
best-known comedy club—the same club where, it seemed
like only yesterday, Ptak had gotten his start playing hip
Dean Martin to Otis King's funky, jive-talking Jerry Lewis.
Or was it white Aykroyd to black Belushi?

I stared at Nathanson, my desire for a safe haven slowly
succumbing to the intense, sometimes almost voyeuristic curiosity that had drawn me to my chosen field in the first
place. There was not likely to have been a more interesting
case in Los Angeles at the moment. And who was to know

how it would really affect my therapy? Besides, I had to admit, there was something oddly appealing about having my shrink in my debt.

"Sure," I said. "I'll do it."

"Good," said Nathanson. "I'll have Emily call you. See you next time."

2

"So you think someone killed your husband."

"I don't think. I ..." Emily Ptak half gasped and gestured futilely through my living room window, the checkerboard pastels of West Hollywood spread out behind it. Emily had insisted we meet at my office/apartment because she wanted anonymity and someplace she could bring her four-year-old daughter, Genevieve. So I stashed Genevieve in my bedroom with the cable TV and found a cup of herb tea for Emily, but she still wasn't really able to articulate. Standing up, she drank a couple of swallows of tea, then placed it on the coffee table and started pacing back and forth between my microfilm reader and the sofa while clenching and unclenching her hands.

"Why don't you sit down a minute?"

"No!"

But she sat, almost primly, on the edge of the sofa. I glanced up from her pink hightops and slightly ill-fitting gray kimono skirt to her dirty blond hair cut short in a punk style that did little to mask her coarse, almost bovine features. Although Emily Ptak had been married to a hip comic, wore trendy Japanese clothes, and was only about twenty-seven, she already had a matronly quality. There was something oddly endearing about that—as if, beneath it all, she desperately wished to dissociate herself from a sophisticated life she didn't want or ask for. But there was also something tight and conservative about it.

"Gene speaks very highly of you."

"Gene?" For a split second I didn't realize whom she was talking about. "You mean Dr. Nathanson?"

"Yes, I've, uh, been seeing him for over two years now." Emily blushed and fidgeted with a pair of Carrera sunglasses she nervously removed from her purse.

"What do you do besides that?"

"You mean for work? I'm an M.S.W., but right now I'm just volunteering a couple of days a week with Cosmic Aid, Eddy Sandollar's foundation in Ojai. He's doing really original work with famine relief. I'd like to do more but ..." She nodded toward the bedroom.

"I understand. And how can I help you?" I asked, sounding more like a parish priest than a detective. Or maybe like Nathanson. Through the window directly behind her a large billboard dominated the Strip, urging SAFE SEX. It showed about a half-dozen muscular, shirtless gay guys grouped around a tiny, smiling Jewish *bubba*. L.A. LOVES YOU LIKE A MOTHER, it read, giving the number of the AIDS hot line. Beyond that another billboard showed a starving African child and said HELP HIM SURVIVE, giving the number of something called the California Hunger Project. This was West Hollywood in the eighties—the Plague Years.

Emily continued to fidget with her Carrera glasses, holding them far away from her body as she folded and unfolded them.

"Mike didn't do it," she said. "He wasn't the suicide type."

"What's the suicide type?"

"He was never depressed, for one thing."

"Really?"

"Really. I know it sounds weird, but he just never let anything get to him. He wasn't particularly good at what he did and that didn't even bother him. He was happy being a straight man." She glanced over at her daughter who was visible through a crack in the bedroom door, staring at the TV with a sad, mechanical expression. "Not like me. I'm a typical endogenous depressive. I'm almost as bad as Gene."

"*He's* depressed?"

"Shrinks are the most depressed people in the world. Who do you think has the highest suicide rate?"

"Yeah, I know," I said. That was all I needed—a depressed shrink. With my luck, it was a communicable disease. "So," I continued, "do you have anything specific about Mike—or is this all based on character analysis?"

She stood and looked away, lost in thought a moment. Then she took out a cigarette and lit it, staring painfully at her matchbook as if it were a symbol of decadence of some kind. It was from the Plaza Athenée in Paris. "Do you know a lot of people in show business?" she asked.

"Sure. You live in Los Angeles half your life, you have to know a lot of them."

"What do you think of them?"

"As a generalization, I think they have a great life. That's why they bitch about it so much. Who else gets to do what they want—more or less—and is paid a fortune for it?"

"Guilt provoking," she said. "Some of them give the pleasure principle such free reign, they don't recognize their death wish until it's too late."

Endogenous depression. Pleasure principle. This woman *had* done a lot of shrinking. At least she knew the buzz words. "What does this have to do with the subject at hand?"

"What do you know?"

"What I read in the *L.A. Times.* They indicated Mike's career was floundering. Three weeks before, his five-year partnership with Otis King had been dissolved. A week after that, King signed a three-picture pact with Global Pictures for six million dollars plus a percentage of profits. That could drive a man to suicide. At least it was good enough for the police. . . . Is this accurate?"

"As far as it goes."

"What else should I know?"

"Otis King is an ambulatory schiz with extreme obsessive-compulsive tendencies."

"What's that supposed to mean?"

"He's a human time bomb. Into everything—coke, heroin, speedballs, freebase, Methedrine, Percodan, men, women, children, transvestites, and dogs."

"Sounds uninhibited."

"He makes Richard Pryor seem like Mother Theresa."

The doorbell rang.

"Just a second," I said, and went and looked through the peephole. My thirteen-year-old son, Simon, was standing there grinning at me in a dirty Clash T-shirt and a pair of ratty cutoffs.

I opened the door a crack and looked at him. "Hey, sport. Good to see you. But come back a little later. It's business hours."

"I know, Dad. But it's an emergency. I gotta have sixteen dollars. Fast."

"Sixteen dollars?" I glanced back at Emily, who had discreetly turned the other way. "What in hell for?"

"Spray paint."

"What're you gonna do? Hit up on somebody's garage door so I have to bail you out of the sheriff's station like I did two weeks ago?"

"Nah, we got permission." He nodded behind him where three of his teen-age buddies were leaning against the corridor wall, trying to look like surly gang members but not quite making it. It was his regular crew, the KGB—the Kings of Graffiti Bombing. For a middle-class white kid, Simon was heavily ghetto-identified and spent his time break-dancing, practicing black and Chicano slang, or spray-painting graffiti. Mostly the latter. The weird thing was, he was very good at it.

"Look, your mother gets child support for this. Besides, you know the law—if I give you the money, they still can't sell it to you. You need an adult to buy spray paint in California."

"Yeah ... that's why I thought maybe you could come with us."

That was it. I took him aside. "Listen, schmuck, can't you see I'm busy? I'm working."

"Dad, I know ... but you gotta understand. We got *special* permission to throw a bomb on a wall by the Pan Pacific."

"Who gave you permission?"

"The Parks Commission dude. And if we don't do it now, we—"

"Did your friends try *their* parents?"

"They can't find 'em. Dad, graffiti's *art*. You said so yourself. Besides, this is a contest. The dudes who do the best pieces get beamed up to New York for the nationals!"

"All right. All right. What a con job! Just wait in the lobby till I'm finished."

"Thanks, Dad. You're fresh." Simon gave me a big hug and rushed off to join his friends. I turned back to Emily.

"Sorry. I got a kid with an identity crisis. He thinks he's a member of the Third World."

But Emily was now sitting back down on the sofa, staring off into space. I walked over to her.

"So what is it?" I said. "You think Otis King is responsible for his own partner's demise?"

"I don't know."

"It doesn't make much sense, considering what's happened to Otis, his good fortune."

"That may be. But whatever happened, I know it's not suicide. And if I don't do something about it ..." She stopped, biting so hard I could see a drop of blood forming at the top of her lip. " ... I don't know how I'll answer to Genevieve when she grows up." She looked over toward my bedroom. The little girl had stopped watching television and was standing in the doorway staring straight at us in a macabre, unblinking way that reminded me for an instant of *The Exorcist*. "How much do you charge, Moses?" But before I could answer she said, "Never mind. I trust you. Just bill me."

All my clients should be that way, I thought.

"How do I get to Otis King?" I asked.

"Not easy. He's trying to kick his drug habit and he's under twenty-four-hour-a-day therapy with Dr. Carl Bannister in the Malibu Colony. Until he's cured, Bannister's keeping him in total isolation. Nobody can get in."

God. Another shrink.

3 "The hidden purpose of psychotherapy is to brainwash people into accepting society as it exists, accommodate them to what is wrong so they can be comfortable with themselves and not want to change things. Isn't that right, Moses?"

"I have the feeling I'd be uncomfortable in any society."

"That's because you're so self-involved. If you'd try to contribute to the welfare of others, you wouldn't spend so much time walking along with a face as long as your arm. Think about the freedom fighters in South Africa, El Salvador ... the new resistance against fascism in Chile ... the strugglers against Soviet social imperialism in Afghanistan. ... By the way—how's your sex life?"

"About half as alive as the Democratic party."

I was with my aunt Sonya, driving east from Venice along Pico Boulevard. It wasn't my normal procedure to bring a septuagenarian on casework, but I had broken my last two dates with her, and I knew if I did it a third time, I'd never hear the end of it.

"And let me add," she said, "that by the welfare of others I do not mean just one particular senior citizen. I mean—"

"I know. I know. 'The greatest good for the greatest number.' Thank you, Jeremy Bentham."

"Thank God you still remember something in this narcissistic culture hell-bent on navel contemplation and acquisition of personal possessions!''

"All right. All right." We were pulling up to the valet parking of the Fun Zone. "Is it all right if I give this exploited worker my BMW or should I park it myself?''

"How else do you expect him to make a living?''

On the east end of the Sunset Strip, the Fun Zone ("the Omphalos of American Comedy") was your basic L.A. Eighties Trendoid Post-Deco club with a dusty rose and gray tile façade and a brushed stainless steel front door that looked like it was borrowed from the engine room of the *Queen Mary*. You drove up to it by a side driveway that cut between the club and a recently built piece of work called the Albergo Picasso, a self-described "European-style spa hotel" done on the exterior in a series of multicolored squares said to derive from the master's Cubist Period and on the interior in "harmonious tones" out of his Blue and Rose periods. It was the kind of place my New York friends would once have used for a facile put-down of L.A. but now would rush to stay in, because with its minimalist cuisine, German cars, and diminishing smog, Los Angeles had become, by attrition, the spiritual capital of today's "material world." And that, as the lady sang, was where we lived.

The heady smell of fame, or at least the dream of it, was the driving motif of the Fun Zone itself. The moment you passed through its steel portals you were in a corridor lined with hundreds of autographed photos of aspiring comics who had performed at the club hoping to land two minutes on Johnny or Merv or—who knew?—maybe even a raunchy comedy for Warner Bros. in which they could strut their stuff in this summer's food fight. As if part of a definite hierarchy, the corridor opened onto a larger lobby decorated with oversize portraits of the greats of comedy from Chaplin to Lenny Bruce. At the opposite end of the lobby, in a place of honor just beside the entrance to the main room (the Fun Zone had three rooms—one for the star attraction, one for the up-and-comers, and a third, called The Combat Zone, for women comics only) was a twelve-foot-high portrait of the God himself, Richard Pryor, the man who had put the club on the map as the place to be in funnyland when he had premiered his first one-man show there almost ten years ago.

Not far from Pryor, and clearly recently installed, was a lesser photograph of Ptak and King. With Mike's corpse only a week in the ground, there were several people standing around eyeing it curiously when Sonya and I stepped forward.

"What a marshmallow," she said, staring right in Ptak's face. I had to admit her evaluation of the soft, fleshy blond man with the slight overbite gazing out from the black and white still was not very different from mine. I had seen Ptak perform once, as a guest on the Letterman show, and didn't think he was particularly funny. He seemed to have less talent than most straight men. He couldn't sing, he couldn't dance, and he certainly couldn't tell a joke. In fact, he was sort of an anachronism, the kind of comic foil that didn't seem necessary in this day and age. King, on the other hand, was like a black, street version of Dennis the Menace, all unbridled id, an uptight white man's worst fantasy turned outrageous—a comic mugger. In the photograph he looked as if he were made of wire, all muscle and bone in sneakers, jeans, tank top, and baseball cap turned around backward.

19

He had a wide grin on his face that defied you to decide whether it was evil or mischievous and so much energy he vibrated off the photograph. He was so magnetic, within a second you forgot Ptak was even up there with him, like so much instant mashed potatoes vanished down a drain.

"Now, *that's* what I call sexy," said Sonya. She wasn't talking about Mike or Otis but about a red-headed woman of about thirty who was visible through the door standing on the stage of The Combat Zone, trying desperately to reach an audience that looked like a combination of bored Vals and tourists from Iowa.

"So," she was saying, "sometimes I think I'm a minority of one. My cause is so obscure I couldn't get a terrorist to kidnap me if I walked naked through the streets of Damascus."

There was a slight ripple of laughter and a tinkling of glasses. The woman shrugged as she reached for a water pitcher. "You know why the Canucks call us Pepsis, don't you? We're half flat, bottled up, and grin like idiots when they step on us."

"What kind of accent is that?" I asked.

"Her? What are you—an idiot? She's a Pepsi. French-Canadian! Don't you read the papers anymore? René Lévesque stepped down. It's the end of the Parti Québecois, the separatist movement. That's what she's talking about."

"Oh." No wonder the Vals weren't laughing. I doubted the Iowans found it very funny either.

I stepped closer to the door and took another look at her. She was dressed elegantly in a simple blue sweater and black leather pants that showed off the kind of slim hips you wanted to slide your arm around and crush into your body. Sonya was right. She was attractive. But right now she didn't look very happy. In fact, she looked like she was laying a first-class El Bombo.

"What're you doing here, Wine? Amateur Night's Monday."

I hadn't seen him in about five years, but I didn't have to look to recognize the voice of Art Koontz of homicide. When I did, however, I was surprised at how good he looked—fifteen pounds lighter, with stylish clothes and a haircut out of *Gentleman's Quarterly.* He used to be a dead ringer for Popeye Doyle in *The French Connection.* These days everybody was going upscale.

"I didn't know you were a friend of comedy, Inspector."

"Everybody likes a few laughs, Wine. Of course, it's hard to keep up with you hippies turned yuppie. You don't know *who's* driving the BMW these days. Is it true that sushi's out—or have I been misinformed by *California* magazine?"

"You don't look like you're doing badly yourself either, Koontz. Nice suit. What is it? Armani?"

"Gianni Versace."

I whistled. "The boys in Parker Center'll think you're on the take, you keep wearing duds like that." He frowned, but I smiled back pleasantly. Actually it was kind of nice to see the old bastard after all this time. And it saved me a trip downtown. He could only have been there for one reason, and as I'm sure he knew, the same was true for me.

"How about a drink?" I pointed to the bar of The Combat Zone where the French-Canadian was still trying gamely to make a dent in her audience. "The Evian's on me. Or do you prefer Pellegrino?"

"Bourbon. Bourbon with *no* water."

I guided him toward the bar before he changed his mind. Sonya was right beside us. Koontz eyed her suspiciously. "This is my aunt Sonya Lieberman."

"Your *aunt?*" He made a face of disbelief and turned to me directly. "Look, I don't know who your client is—though I could guess. But if you're out to make a murder case, I can tell you straight off the bat, forget it. Ptak did this all by himself."

I had to agree it certainly looked that way. According to the papers, he had checked into the penthouse suite at six-oh-five that evening and took the elevator directly upstairs. At precisely nine-thirty-two, three hours and twenty-seven minutes later, he was on his way down by the express route. The elevator gave directly onto the suite foyer and the operator, a Mr. Sanchez, insisted he brought no one up or down between those times. Furthermore, the bellhop, a Mr. Nastase, said that, as far as he knew, no one was in the suite when he escorted Mr. Ptak up with one suitcase. And he had made a relatively complete survey of the premises since Ptak wanted a guided tour of all the perks of the suite (projection TV with VCR and quadraphonic stereo, grand piano, bar and gourmet kitchen, billiard table, etc.) and Nastase, the *Los Angeles Times* reported, was eager to get as large a tip as possible from the show business fat cat. Of course there was the question of the emergency exit, but the fire door to the back stairs of the penthouse had to be opened by a key and all those keys were either in the possession of the hotel management or of Ptak, who had his in his jacket pocket when he plunged to his death.

Our drinks arrived and I paid for them with my VISA card. "Thanks for the drink, Wine," said Koontz. "I imagine you're being paid well, but do us both a favor and get out of this case. Go get yourself a nice personal injury job, a dentist in a Maserati, and bag this one. The lady—and I know it's a lady— who hired you is just dealing with her own psychological problems, which might be bad, but weren't half as bad as her husband's. There's nothing you can find out for her that will please her in any way, and there are no guilty parties to this crime, if you can call it that, other than the man's own sad life. And I'm sure an educated person like you would agree, each of us has the right to take his own life. Unless you've suddenly gone religious on me."

"Not me, Koontz. I'm a card-carrying atheist, except for two years with Rajneesh when he was still in the business. But tell me, if this is all so simple, what the hell are you doing here?" I didn't sound as decisive as I wanted to. I was having trouble keeping my eyes off the French-Canadian. Her teeth were crooked and her nose was too big, but there was something about her. Maybe, as the Jungians would say, she touched my anima. Or maybe she was just sexy as hell. Whatever it was, she gave me the kind of knot in my stomach I hadn't felt in years. Unfortunately for her, the audience didn't feel the same way. At this point they were booing her unmercifully. Some wit in the first row was telling her to eat frogs' legs and hop back to Montreal.

"Well, Wine, I might as well tell you, since an idiot in

the DA's office leaked it to the *Times* this morning anyway: your friend Ptak was wired to the ceiling when he flew out of the window of the Picasso last week. He was so fucked up on speedballs he probably thought he was Captain Marvel. . . . Sorry, ma'am.''

"I'm aware of speedballs, Inspector," said Sonya sharply. "And not from senior citizens' bowling. Heroin and cocaine. Two parts blow and three parts skag, depending on who's mixing.''

"Yeah, right," Koontz mumbled sheepishly.

The French-Canadian left the stage to scattered applause, except for mine, and I turned back fullface to the two of them. "So it's Hollywood-and-drugs time, the big career-maker in L.A. law enforcement. You guys could really get some action out of this, another Belushi case. No wonder the little DA leaked it. What's he after—city council or a judge-ship?''

"There's not going to be another Belushi case," Koontz said icily. "This time we're going to put a stop to this, find the source of this business and stamp it out.''

"Ah, c'mon, Koontz. Don't give me this single source crap. You get drugs in this town twenty-six ways to Brooklyn. You know that better than I do. You worked Rampart for fifteen years. They've got more dealers down there than they've got taco stands.''

"Down there isn't the entertainment industry. And in this case, it's not Brooklyn. It's the Bronx.'' He held his drink to his chest and leaned closer to me. "We have information that a certain individual on the other side of this country is attempting to corner the drug market on an extremely affluent, indeed unbelievably affluent, sector of our society. And as you know, that sector has immense influence on the minds and morals of our children, indeed on the minds and morals of children all over the world. Now, the presence of a private eye muddying the waters over one measly suicide that's already over and done with can only complicate a crucial investigation. So I ask you as a citizen and as a family man to get out!''

"I can't get out, Koontz. I promised someone I'd do this."

"Who?"

"My shrink."

"Your shrink? ... Jesus, you were better off when you were a pinko!''

He slammed down his drink and marched off.

4 I sat there with Sonya for a few minutes, then left her watching a pair of women twin comics (the Non-Identicals) making weird incest jokes and went outside to reconnoiter. Ptak had landed somewhere near the back of the Fun Zone, and I found the remnants of a police circle when I walked around the corner by the stage door. I stared down at the fading chalk, looking from the black asphalt up to the penthouse terrace from which he supposedly jumped. It had a low white stucco wall that looked easy to climb over, even to fall over. I stepped into the center of the ring and tried to reconstruct his movements in my mind's eye, but there was something about suicide that made me recoil from contemplating it. I was wondering whether that was normal behavior or whether that was just me, when I heard what sounded like a dry heave. I turned toward the stage door to see the French-Canadian leaning out with one hand clutching the doorframe. She didn't look embarrassed when she saw me.

"It was a disaster," she said.

I nodded sympathetically.

"Worse. A catastrophe. I'm quitting right now. It's all over. Never again. Only a self-destructive moron does something they're no good at. Did you know I used to be a laboratory technician? I was once a photographer. Also a disc jockey in Gaspé. Why I decided to be a comedian, I'll never know." Then she bent over and tried to throw up again, but nothing came out. "Jesus, do you have a Certs or something?"

"Sorry, I—"

"Don't worry about it.... God, you're standing in the bull's-eye. Another depressed comic bites the dust. I'm not superstitious or anything, but if I were you, I'd get the hell out of there." I stepped out of the circle toward her. "What a mess!" she continued. Her accent was much fainter off-stage, but she had the same slim hips and gorgeous red hair. "Comedians really are total nut cases. They'd be pathetic if they weren't such clichés. It's just like *Pagliacci*. '*Ridi del duol che t'avvelena il cor!*'"

"What's that mean?"

"'Laugh at the sorrow which is poisoning your heart!' I told you I was a disc jockey. What a job *that* was—midnight to four A.M. playing opera for lumberjacks. Maybe I just don't stick to things."

"Maybe you're restless."

"You know what I should be?" She nodded with conviction. "A private detective."

I burst out laughing.

"What's so funny?"

"You wouldn't like it."

"How would you know?"

"Oh, I know."

"What makes you so sure?"

"I probably know more about it than anybody you've ever met."

She eyed me cooly. "I see. . . . Well, good-bye."

She started off.

"Hey, where're you going?"

"I don't like people who make assumptions about other people, even if they *are* private eyes, which you must be, because if you're not, you're the most egocentric person I've ever met. Besides, you're obviously here looking into Mike Ptak's death."

"Assumption on your part."

"Furthermore," she continued without bothering to contradict me, "if you were any good at what you did, you'd want to interview me."

"I would? Why's that?"

"I was standing right here when it happened."

"You were?"

"That's right. I was pacing around back here before going on, trying to remember my jokes, or maybe trying to forget them, when I heard someone scream something and then I saw him come flying down.''

"Scream something? Scream what?''

"I'm not sure. Something like 'nestral' or 'nestron' or 'neuter.' ''

" 'Neuter'?''

"Weird, huh? Anyway, it was something like that. My English sounds good, but it isn't perfect. Did you ever try to perform in a foreign language? It's no picnic. Of course it's not half so bad as seeing somebody's guts splattered across the asphalt like yesterday's chicken salad.''

"Did you tell the police about this?''

"Yes, of course. It's no secret. I've told the police and now I've told you, Mr. ...''

"Wine. Moses Wine.''

"Yes. Mr. Wine ... good night.'' She started off again.

"Wait a minute.''

"I really need some Certs, Mr. Wine.''

"I'd like to see you again.''

"What for?''

"I don't know. The usual thing. Single divorced male seeks attractive redhead with sense of humor and checkered employment history for fun and—''

"Oh.'' She looked disappointed. "I thought it was because you might need help with your case. I was serious about being a private detective. I'm even taking a course at the Learning League. Good-bye.''

She disappeared into the club.

I decided to extend Sonya's comedy education a bit longer and pay a visit to the Albergo Picasso.

I entered through the front door and crossed directly through the main lobby, past some imitation African masks and a full-size reproduction of *Guernica,* to the concierge's desk. A tall blond guy in his late twenties wearing a dark suit with the traditional crossed keys was standing behind it with a bored expression. He looked like a surfer who went to finishing school.

"How do you do? My name's Mark Burg," I told him. "I'm co-owner of Second Skin Leathers down in Redondo Beach. Do you know it?"

He didn't open his mouth.

"I guess you don't. Anyway, we specialize in quality leathers like this." I gestured to my own jacket, which I had picked up on sale in the Mexico City flea market. "Also lizard skins, ostrich, and other endangered species. Did you ever see an anaconda belt?"

"No." He seemed slightly more interested.

"They look great with our skintight virgin fawn pants. Some people get their own turquoise Navajo buckle to go with it, but I think they're a little passé. Don't you agree?"

"Yeah."

"Anyway, we've got some *very important* vendors coming in from Milan with all the latest styles and—you know Redondo Beach—it's not exactly happening down there. So we naturally thought of a bungalow at the Beverly Hills, but my partner said I just *had* to see the penthouse at the Picasso."

"The penthouse is closed."

"Really? Until when?"

"Further notice."

"Remodeling?"

"Police matter."

"Ah-ha. Well, look, these guys are gonna be here in six weeks. Surely it'll be open by then. And they need a nice large suite. Somewhere they can keep all their samples. They always have a lot of extras lying around. And they love to give them away to the staff. It makes them feel like big tippers. And you know Europeans—they think the concierge is a big deal." I let that sit there, but not too long. "What's your name, sir?"

"Edward Lomax."

"Do you think I could have a look at the penthouse, Mr. Lomax? If the police have it locked up, there's no one in there now."

"Yeah, I suppose," he said, trying to suppress a smile at all the great gear he'd be collecting. First Koontz, now this one. Everyone in Los Angeles had gone berserk for clothes or food.

He rang for the bellhop. "Nastase!"

A squat man with a shaven head and a mottled body alternately layered with muscle and fat instantly materialized from behind a pillar. A crucifix dangled from his neck and his breath smelled faintly of garlic, giving him, despite the requisite "Blue Period" tunic, the appearance of a refugee from a photograph of some old Greco-Roman wrestling competition. He seemed so outrageously out of place in this determinedly with-it environment that I had to be careful to restrain myself from laughing.

"Show Mr. Burg the D'Avignon Suite," said Lomax, handing him the key.

Nastase didn't say a word until we were halfway up in the

elevator. "Is you a religious gentleman, mister?" He had a thick Eastern European accent.

"Funny, you're the second guy to ask me that tonight. No, I'm not particularly religious ... but I see you are." I nodded to his crucifix. "I bet you're Romanian Orthodox."

"Yes, yes!" he said proudly. "How you know that, mister?"

"Nastase, like Nastase, the great Romanian tennis player."

"Yes, yes. Very great. He Ilie Nastase. I Vasile Nastase." The elevator opened on the penthouse suite. "Vasile Nastase from Moldavia. Near place you Americans know very good—Transylvania!" He laughed as if this were a huge joke, then suddenly looked grave as we took a step forward into the foyer of the D'Avignon Suite. Not surprisingly, a reproduction of Picasso's famous *Demoiselles* was staring us straight in the face as we entered. Nastase dropped to his knees and crossed himself. "This sad place, mister."

"Yeah," I said. "I heard. Some comedian committed suicide here the other week." I walked into the living room while Nastase lurked in the doorway. It seemed as if the police investigation had been completed. The usual warnings about evidence-tampering were gone and everything was meticulously turned out like a normal hotel room between guests. If there had been any indications of struggle, they were long gone. I continued into the bedroom, Nastase shuffling reluctantly behind me as if Dracula's own curse were in the air. "But I'm not superstitious, are you?"

"The Romanian Orthodox Church is autocephalous, mister."

"Autocephalous?"

"Not under jurisdiction of other church. Has own bishop in Bucharest even under Communists."

"What does that have to do with superstition?" I walked out onto the balcony.

"No. Don't go there. Is bad place."

I ignored him and went over to the balcony rail, glancing up from Ptak's grim destination to the glittering view that went straight down La Cienega past Baldwin Hills to the airport. Then I turned back to Vasile, whose bull-like Greco-Roman presence was lurking at the balcony entrance. "Where were you when it happened?"

"I not here," he said flatly.

"Well, that's good. Fellow like that falls off a building, I imagine the police would ask a lot of questions."

"They ask, but so what?"

"Yeah, so what? If you're not here, you're not here. Where *were* you then?"

"Why you ask?" He took a step toward me.

"Curiosity. I'm in the leather business and I'm interested in people's motivations. For sales."

"Well, I not here. I tell you. I not like your questions, mister. How you know so much about Romania?"

"I don't know much about Romania. All I know are Nastase and Nadia Comaneci."

Vasile didn't look appeased. He took another step toward me. I walked past him back inside, just to be on the safe side.

"One other question. My business partners—they're very

nervous about fire. How do you get out of here, in case of an emergency?"

Vasile came back in and unbolted the fire door without comment. It led down a dark industrial stair.

"Pretty spooky in there," I said. "Suppose you're playing around back there, you know, just for fun, and you get stuck. Can you get back in?"

"Then you stupid," he said.

5 "The French-Canadian? Her name is Chantal Barrault."

"Barreled?"

"Not Barreled, you illiterate. Bah-row. Like Jean-Louis Barrault, the great movie star from the Golden Age of the Cinema."

"Before Cheech and Chong?"

"Smart guy. Always a smart guy. Maybe you *should* be in therapy, the way you always mask your aggressive feelings in a wise remark." I had been driving Sonya back to the senior citizens center, listening to her evaluations of the various comics. "That's what the rest of them do, attack the audience like that dreadful Rivers woman or make stupid jokes about cocaine. Cocaine has replaced mothers-in-law as the major source of humor. Whatever happened to Lenny Bruce? Now, *there* was a man. By the way, you might be interested to know there's a big competition between the Fun Zone and that other comedy club, Joysville."

"I think we're being followed."

"Really?" Sonya brightened. I knew she'd like that. What the hell—at seventy-three you might as well have a little action in your life. There aren't that many more chances. "How do you know?"

"The car behind us has its right headlight out."

"Yeah? So?"

"At the last stoplight it had its left one out."

"You mean they switch 'em back and forth?"

"With a little gizmo under the dash. It's kind of a rolling disguise."

"Clever, clever."

"Not clever enough for us, though, was it?" I pulled into a mini-mall, parking right in front of a brightly lit 7-Eleven. "Sit tight."

"Sure thing, Bull Drummond."

Bull Drummond? *That* was from the Golden Age of the Nickelodeon. I got out of the car and walked into the liquor store, then went straight out the back way without even a sideways glance at the irritated clerks. Outside, I quickly pulled an old baseball cap out of my hip pocket and a pair of nonprescription horn-rimmed glasses and moved quickly around the block, crossing the boulevard at the next light.

As I expected, a somewhat battered cream-colored Toyota was parked about forty yards down at the proper vantage point to see all the exits from the mini-mall. A hefty dark-haired guy in his fifties, probably an ex-cop, was seated in the driver's seat, tapping impatiently on the steering wheel.

I approached casually, made a mental note of his license plate, then crossed the street about thirty feet from his car, returning to the back of the 7-Eleven, where I took off the hat and glasses, bought a sixpack of Harvey Weinhard (with a receipt for Emily Ptak), and returned to the car. The Toyota followed me all the way out to Venice and then back to West Hollywood after I had dropped off Sonya. It remained outside my apartment for a half hour. By then it was one-thirty. I turned off my lights and went to sleep.

The next morning I called my DMV contact to check out the Toyota. It usually took him about fifteen minutes to get back to me with his packet of information, so I made myself some coffee and stared out my kitchen window down the Strip past the same billboards for AIDS and the California Hunger Project. About a mile off, the Astro House glowed gold in the morning light. A classic Art Deco mini-scraper from the twenties with a spire like the Chrysler Building and a site that dominated half of Los Angeles, it had fallen on bad times, its original bas-reliefs flaking and its ornate windows boarded up or smashed. If someone ever bothered to fix it up, it would've been a masterpiece. But in this era of dying gays and starving Africans, I wouldn't have given it top priority.

The Toyota, a 1973 Corolla, was the fully owned and sole vehicle of one Stanley Burckhardt. He had one moving violation for running a stop sign in 1984 and was listed on 2380 Sixth Street in Los Angeles. I dialed him straight off.

The phone answered: "Peace of Mind Insurance. Can I help you?"

I hung up immediately. Peace of Mind Insurance. Obviously one of my colleagues and, just as obviously, a specialist in unsavory domestic matters—divorce, adultery, X-rated motel surveillance—everything, in short, that makes a private eye feel like a seedy schmuck. This was going to be easier than I thought.

I pulled up in front of Burckhardt's office about a half hour later. It was on a run-down part of Sixth just shy of the Miracle Mile district, as if whatever saint decreed such matters had said, "The miracle stops here!" and the blocks and blocks of shiny mirrored high-rises were suddenly interrupted by a 1915 vintage lump of neo-Victorian sooty brick called the Fallbrook Arms. My son Simon and his buddies could have improved it with a little graffiti.

I ignored the flaking plaster and urine-scented corridors and marched directly up to Burckhardt's office on the fourth floor, barging in on him so quickly he didn't have a chance to get his maple bar out of his mouth and put away his copy of *Penthouse Forum*.

"What's the matter?" I said. "Couldn't you afford someone for your morning run or were they just better than you are? You know, some of us *work* in the daytime. In fact, some of us work at libraries or at the courthouse or the registrar of voters or the Hall of Records. Of course, some of us don't work at all!" I was pouring out a lot of vitriol at this small-time loser and I didn't particularly like it. It had the acrid smell of self-hate.

"I don't know what you're talking about," he managed.

"Oh, c'mon, Burckhardt, you know exactly what I'm talking about. Now, who put you up to this or do you want to be slapped with an invasion of privacy suit?"

"Oh, Jesus. Give a guy a break. You're in this business too. Of course, lookin' at that car you drive, you must be makin' out a lot better than I am."

"That's last year's car. Now look, I don't know what you know about this, but this isn't some Armenian deli owner trying to juggle three mistresses and an ex-wife. Someone could have been murdered here and I'm sure you don't want to be mixed up in a capital crime, particularly on the killer's side. So I'm going to make you a simple proposition: you tell me who hired you to watch me and I'll pretend it never happened . . . and I'll pay you besides."

"How much?"

"Two hundred dollars." What the hell, it was Emily's money.

"Not enough. You can't buy me, mister! Who d'ya think I am?"

"Two-fifty."

"All right." He looked away quickly in embarrassment. I was almost embarrassed myself. "Only I don't know the guy's name."

"You don't know your client's name?"

"I was about to close up last night . . ." Close up, I thought. It was the safest bet in California that this guy slept on the couch behind me. " . . . when this kid comes in all nervous and excited. He must've been about twenty-two, twenty-three, and real skinny, but I don't think he was a hype." For a moment I didn't realize he meant an addict. This guy *was* back in the 1940s. "He's got this car what's parked around the Fun Zone he wants me to follow—a BMW with your plate numbers—and tell him everything about who owns it and whatever. He offers me sixty-five on the spot and a hundred more when I got the information and tells me to send it all care of B and B, post office box such and such in Glendale.''

"B and B, like the after-dinner drink?''

"Yeah, that's what I thought. Only the minute I mention it he gets all upset, like he wouldn't have nothin' to do with alcohol, as if I was gonna offer him a swig of my Gordon's Extra Dry over there.'' He nodded toward a half-empty bottle of generic gin on an end table. "Anyway, I had it wrong. It was B *for* B, not B *and* B.''

Great, I thought. That clarified matters.

"So the kid just slips me the sixty-five and runs out of here like a scared coyote on Wilshire Boulevard. Ever seen that—a coyote on Wilshire Boulevard? I did once. The day before Eisenhower was elected. So that's my story, Maury. More than that I can't tell you. I guess it's not worth the full two-fifty, but ...''

I stood there a moment before continuing. Somehow just being in this room was giving me a headache. "Stanley, you're a professional in this business.''

"Uh-huh. Sure. Twenty-six years.''

"You and I both know getting a P.O. box identity out of the Glendale post office is about as easy as doing a tooth extraction on a Bengal tiger.''

"Yeah, yeah. Right.'' He liked that one.

"So I've got a proposition for you.'' I reached into my wallet for a crisp hundred-dollar bill. "I'm giving you this hundred now to go over to the Glendale post office and stake out that box. There's a hundred more in it for each additional day it takes you and a five-hundred-buck bonus when you tell me whose box it is.''

"Sounds great to me, pal. I'm your man.''

It was a close race between Burckhardt and me to see who was out the door first. I felt better the moment I hit the street. It was a gorgeous day in early October, my favorite time of year in L.A., and the opening day of the new California Lottery. I went into the liquor store across the street and bought a ticket. It was kind of a bingo game and you had to get three of a kind to win. The first two numbers were $5,000.00, but the next four chances came up trumps when I scratched them off. I put it down to not-a-bad-start and got back into my car. In any case, I was off to Malibu to see Otis King, and just the thought of being near the ocean kept me in a good mood. On the way I stopped by the phone company's phone book library on Wilshire just to see if something resembling B for B popped up. There wasn't anything similar in the L.A. directories for the last five years. I also knew I should check the fictitious business name listings in the courthouse building on Hill Street, but it was sheer drudgery and I wished I had someone I could trust to do that. Sometimes I used my older son, Jacob, but he was in school now, getting ready for his college boards on Saturday.

It was then I thought of Chantal Barrault. Maybe she was serious about being a PI. One trip down to the court would cure her. Anyway, a woman like that would be crazy to have a listed phone number. I checked anyway. She wasn't crazy.

I kept thinking of Chantal Barrault as I drove out to Malibu. She only started to drift out of my mind as I came through the tunnel leading from the Santa Monica Freeway onto the Pacific Coast Highway. The minute I got down by the water, I always wondered why I didn't live there. Maybe it was fear of isolation, not living in the middle of things in West Hollywood, the newly incorporated capital of gay pride, gray power, and fresh lox. But I often thought that if I had someone to live with again, I would move out here, find a spot in those Malibu hills that look so much like Portugal, and watch the whales go by.

I certainly didn't have fantasies about living in that world-famous *cordon sanitaire*—the Malibu Colony. We all have our own level of ambition and mine just didn't run to living in a cluster of 110 $2 million-and-up houses with twenty-eight tennis courts.

Actually, like most things, the Colony was no longer what it once was—the seaside capital of movie glamour. The vicissitudes of the entertainment industry being what they are, some of the more expensive homes had been sold to jet-set refugees and petrodollar riffraff from places like Iran and Saudi Arabia. Now, with oil prices plunging, some of them would doubtless have to move on, to be replaced by whom? I wasn't sure.

I was musing on this subject as I drove up to the Colony gatehouse, which seemed to be modeled after those other imposing edifices that blocked the way into the movie studios themselves. In fact, it was just as easy to get into the Colony as onto a studio lot. All you needed was a knowing look, a fancy car, and perhaps the name and address of someone living within. I often thought it would be fun to put on a Fila jogging suit, rent one of those new Mercedes station wagons, park right on the narrow street that divides the pricier beachfront houses from the less costly landward properties, and start ripping off Mondrians while waving to my friends and neighbors.

Dr. Carl Bannister lived in 63A, a two-story redwood and glass structure on the landward side. The maxed-out funk of the Jesse Johnson Review was pounding through the walls at megadecibels on what must've been studio JBLs or Altecs when I approached. I banged extra hard on the door to be heard over the sonic boom, but a muscular young man of about twenty in a Banana Republic T-shirt opened it almost immediately, as if he had been standing there waiting for me. I glanced up at the video camera above the door and knew why.

"I'm looking for Dr. Carl Bannister," I said, knowing I'd have to see the man himself before I had a chance to see his patient.

"Do you have an appointment?"

"No, I don't. But this is sort of an important matter and—"

"Dr. Bannister is with a patient now."

"That's okay. I'll wait."

"That could be a long while. Sometimes he's with his patients four or five hours at a time."

I nodded. "I'll wait."

The young man looked unhappy. He wasn't losing me as easily as he expected. Behind him I could see a woman walk by in a bikini with a note pad, a Malibu secretary.

"What'd you say your name was?"

"Wine. Moses Wine."

"Why don't you give me your phone number, Mr. Wine, and I'll have the doctor call you?"

"I'd prefer to wait."

I got my foot in the door just before he tried to shut it on me, and I wedged my way into the living room. I had barely taken in the two-story space with the sunken fire pit when a man in his fifties entered wearing a worn pair of khaki shorts, huarache sandals, and no shirt. He had curly silver hair like spun wire à la Joseph Heller or Norman Mailer, but his physique was trimmer. And his piercing, almost catlike hazel eyes gave him the charismatic appearance of a high-toned hypnotist.

"Dad," said the Banana Republic shirt. "This is Mr. Wine."

"Moses Wine," I said.

"Oh, yes, the famous detective. I've heard all about you from friends in the personnel behavior department at Tulip Computers. They were sorry to lose you. It's an honor." He bowed to me with an ambiguous flourish. "No doubt you're here to speak with Otis about the horrible business with Mike."

"If you don't mind."

"Not at all. Not at all. Although if you wish to see Otis alone, that's going to be hard. He can't be alone for six months or so."

"Never?"

"Not according to his contract. From his first jog in the morning until the last late show at night, one of our people is going to be with him. And if he wakes up in the middle of the night, I insist that they call me.'' Bannister gestured toward his son and the secretary.

''You mean his movie contract specifies he can't be alone?''

''No, no.'' The secretary signaled Bannister, who went to answer a blinking phone. ''His contract with me—for the initiation phase of therapy. You lead a person to independence by first making him dependent.'' Bannister picked up. ''Carl, here. Yes, Ian . . . I see. . . . Well, just do what normal people do and go from aisle to aisle in the lot until you've *found* your car. . . . Yes, call me back.'' He hung up and turned to me. ''Celebrities are so sheltered, you have to teach them to walk all over again. . . . C'mon, let's have some lunch—*with* Otis.''

He led me down a corridor toward a mirrored room where the sound of Jesse Johnson was, if anything, redoubled. Otis King was inside working on a rowing machine while a large Polynesian who looked like a bodyguard for the king of Samoa sat sleepily in a wicker chair.

Otis jumped up the moment he saw Bannister. ''Carl, please, baby, my man, my lord, my mother, please please please. . . . The dude called from the California-Hunger-Africa shit and wants me to do a Jerry Lewis on their motherfuckin' telethon. Can I do it, Carl, please? I wanna help them babies, please please please.'' He got down on his knees and begged like a little child.

Bannister went and turned down the stereo. ''Sure, Otis, why not? I want you to help the babies.'' He petted Otis's shoulder as you would a dog. ''This is Moses Wine. He's a private eye looking into Mike's suicide.''

"Oh, man, I don' wanna run down *that* shit again. Blue-jays had me up three days on that one. Almos' set me back in therapy six years. Any more o' that, I'll be a regressive motherfucker, back on the floor like one o' them fetuses." He balled himself up and rolled over by way of demonstration. Then he looked up at us, grinning.

"Good show, Otis," said Bannister.

"Yeah, how you like that body language? Not bad, huh? Pryor never did shit like that. Not even Eddie." He stood up and brushed himself off. "When's lunch? I wanna get me some of that Malipussy!"

"So you one of them private eye mother-fuckers. Get you laid a lot?"

We were sitting in a booth in the Malibu Pharmacy and Otis definitely had his eye on the "Malipussy" as he spoke—and not just the blond, blue-eyed kind, but on anything that walked between the ages of seven and seventy.

"Now and again," I said.

"Yeah? All James Bond gotta do is *look* at it and he get *his* pecker wet. Think I'm a movie star, I could get laid any-time I wanted it. No wonder I'm into coke. . . . C'mere, you!" Otis reached unsuccessfully for a surf bunny who was wandering by in a Malibu Beach Club tank top. She stopped and gave him a look. "Sorry, baby, you know us niggers. We be full-moon crazy we get near the water." He turned back to me with a grin on his face. "So, Magnum-motherfucker, you wanna know 'bout Brother Ptak. I got a suspicion Sigmund here killed him jus' so he could get his greedy little hands on my con-tract—and I ain't talkin' 'bout that shrink contract he made wid me. I'm talkin' 'bout the big-assed cinematic movie star multipic pact, know what I mean? Right, Sigmund?"

He pointed a French fry straight at Bannister, who was sitting beside me, his head profiled against a production still of John Wayne and Montgomery Clift in *Red River*. The Malibu Pharmacy stayed close to its roots.

"I didn't know you were planning on making me your manager," he said.

"Well, you tol' me yo'self I can't let them blowhead mo'fuckers in the Bronx do it no more. They gonna snort my profits or send 'em to Colombia to one of them generals in the green glasses, buy 'em another plantation, and I'll be a lost motherfucker without a penny to my name, rollin' in the gutter all alone. I'm a little lost boy and I need help. Take care of me, take care of me, please please please. You gonna be my main man, right, please?"

"Of course, Otis. Of course I'll be your main man." Ban-nister said it soothingly, as if they were the key words in a mantra. "I'll always be your main man."

Otis calmed down for a second.

It felt like the energy level of the whole room went down a few notches.

"Moses is going to ask you a few questions now," Bannis-ter continued, his voice still sounding like a disc jockey on an easy-listening station.

"Okay, okay," said Otis.

"Where were you when Mike died, Otis?"

"Where I always be," he answered simply. "Right here with Dr. Bannister."

"In the house?"

"Yeah. In the house. We was watchin' a tape of *Road Warrior*. You like that movie?"

"Uh-huh."

"You my *man!* Crazy bald motherfuckers with chains. I love it! ... Anyway, you was askin' me about my alibi. You doin' an interrogation, huh?"

"Yeah."

"Okay, great. I tell you everything you want to know. Is that okay, Doctor?"

"Sure it's okay, Otis," said Bannister.

"When did Mike start on speedballs?"

"Speedballs? He was into *speedballs?* I didn't know that." He turned to Bannister. "See what I mean? I was his partner and I didn't know *shit.* Motherfucker wouldn't tell me nothin'. Probably a racist motherfucker, if you ask me. All that shit about discoverin' me in Washington Square Park when I was doin' stand-up and makin' my career—that's bullshit. Every motherfucker in the Village knew me. Every last hippie and homo. *Even* Swami X knew me ... knew my whole family, even my brother, knew 'em all ... thems that was alive, anyway."

"Who's Swami X?"

"Greatest fuckin' genius of comedy ever was. Learned everything I knew from Swami X. Tell the truth to the motherfuckers. That'll make 'em laugh. Tell 'em their secrets.

Like every motherfucker in this room's thinkin' about pussy—*right now*—whether they like it or not. Whether they *know* it or not. Isn't that right, Doctor?"

"That's right, Otis."

"And if they not thinkin' about pussy, they thinkin' about dick." Suddenly Otis stopped his tirade and looked at me quite seriously. "Who told you Mike was doin' speedballs?"

"Police."

"Motherfuckin' liars."

"How do you know that?"

He jumped up and started pointing at me. "I know it! Don't tell me I don't know it! Who the fuck you think you're tellin'? I was his partner. I fuckin' went on the road with that white nobody. I *made* him. He couldn't make a motherfucker laugh if he tied him down and tickled his dick with ostrich feathers!" Otis sat down again and started muttering. By now everyone in the coffee shop was staring at us openly. "And him always telling me what to do like he was my mother. You my mother, right, Doctor?"

"Yes, Otis."

"Thank God, I got a mother." He looked at me. "You got any more questions, Mr. Dick? I got time for one more question before I take my nap and go to my aerobics class. Gots to be all rested up so's I can get my nose in the bush o' the Nazi bitch teaches that class."

"Okay. Just one. Did you or Mike know anything about a police investigation into drugs in Hollywood? Some big connection back East who's been funneling major amounts of dope to movie people?"

"Connections? What you talkin' about connections?" He

stared at me with a sudden blast of cold hatred. "Who brought him in here?" he said to Bannister.

"He's working for Emily."

"*That* mind-fuckin' cunt.... Look, man, you don't know nothin' about nothin'. Understand? And people who don't know nothin', when they hear somethin', they ain't gonna understand it anyway. So if I was you, I'd take your white face and get as far away from here as you possibly can or one black brother's gonna cut your ass. And that ain't *no joke* from Otis King. That's the blues and the abstract truth. Good-bye, Mr. Charlie." And with that he stood up. "C'mon, Sigmund."

"Good afternoon, Mr. Wine," said Bannister, and followed the black man out. It was hard to know if the tail was wagging the dog or the other way around.

"Bannister *is* directive."

"Otis can't pee without his permission. Every hour of the patient's day is accounted for."

"That must cost a considerable amount."

"Enough to keep a staff of three on twenty-four-hour-a-day duty in a house in the Malibu Colony."

Nathanson shook his head gravely. I was in his office for my usual session that afternoon between two and three. A harsh light filtered in through his greenhouse window and I was feeling uneasy, disoriented. I wasn't sure whether to talk about myself or talk about the case, so the conversation vacillated uncomfortably between the two until the subject of Bannister came up and Nathanson pounced on it like a hawk.

"And on top of everything," I continued, "it's possible that Bannister's real objective is not to cure Otis but to get his hooks into his lucrative career. Otis practically said as much when we were having lunch."

"And do you believe him?"

"I don't know what to believe. Otis is pretty crazy. Or at least he pretends to be. . . . Look, Doctor, I'm still feeling pretty depressed myself. I've been having these dreams about my father and I—"

"Bannister's manipulative. He's more interested in being a guru than a psychiatrist. And he does have excessive material ambitions."

I stared at Nathanson. In the months I had seen him, he had broken his shrink's persona once or twice, but never this severely. It disturbed me and I told him so.

"Well, I'm sorry to hear that," he replied.

"Yes, but this is my hour."

"And?"

"I'm not feeling great."

"And you expect me to solve that for you?"

"You're my shrink!"

"Moses, I am not usually a fan of Carl Jung. But he wrote something once that I thought quite succinct: 'Neurosis is always a substitute for legitimate suffering.' Keep that in mind the next time you expect someone else to solve your problems for you."

"What're you talking about?" I felt a hot stab of anger through the back of my neck. "Then what'm I doing here?"

"Think about it." Nathanson checked his clock. "I'm sorry. That's all we have time for today." He pressed his servo-control and sat up straight.

I got up to leave. "Oh, I meant to ask you—King called Emily Ptak a 'mind-fucking cunt.' Do you know why that was?"

The doctor hesitated. "If I knew, I couldn't give you that information, Moses. She's my patient."

"According to the law, if a psychiatrist has information pertaining to a capital crime, he must reveal it."

"Yes, to the police. You're a private detective. Besides, if you have a question about Emily, I suggest you ask her yourself. See you Thursday."

Thursday? I walked out of Nathanson's office not knowing *what* to think. A good working definition of a schizophrenic was a private detective trying to solve a case for his shrink.

I thought about talking to Emily, but I had something else on my mind as I pulled into a liquor store about half a block away to use the phone. I picked up a couple of lottery tickets while I was making change and started to scratch off the numbers as I walked into the booth. I dialed Parker Center and asked for Inspector Koontz. He wasn't in, but I was redirected to a Sergeant Estrada in homicide who was working on the Ptak case.

"Who's this?" he said. He sounded belligerent.

"Moses Wine. I'm a PI on the Ptak case. I'm a friend of Koontz's." I stretched it a little.

"Yeah."

"He was going to find out for me the hours on that Romanian bellhop, Vasile Nastase—the one who brought Ptak up to his room. I understand his shift was over about twenty minutes after Ptak arrived."

"What'd you say your name was?"

The first card was another loser and I chucked it in the basket.

"Wine."

"Well, Mr. Wine, I wouldn't be going around asking questions about Mr. Nastase if I were you."

"Why's that?" I rubbed through the first two numbers of the second card—one five hundred and a one thousand.

"Because Mr. Nastase turned up dead this morning at about ten-twenty-five."

He hung up. I stuffed the second ticket in my pocket and left.

I got back in my car and started heading east along Sunset back into the city, wondering what I had contributed to Nastase's death. I must have been one of the last to see him alive and he obviously wasn't pleased to see me poking around the D'Avignon Suite at ten o'clock last night. It was obvious too that this would reawaken, and perhaps broaden, the police investigation of Mike Ptak's suicide. Where would they look? On the face of it Nastase, the Romanian Orthodox bellhop, was not a prime candidate for a major participant in the drug world, but then neither was the Thai grandmother I read they arrested last year importing seventy pounds of brown heroin from Bangkok in her husband's funeral urn.

It was almost five o'clock when I reached the Beverly Hills

Hotel, and on an impulse I took a quick left up Benedict Canyon to the address Emily Ptak had left me. She lived in a gated mock-Tudor estate at the end of West Wanda and I parked right in front of it. I was about to press the intercom button when I noticed Genevieve playing in the front yard. I called to her and the little girl ran over, followed immediately by a nervous English nanny, whose concern was only mollified somewhat when she realized the girl knew me. I never got inside the gate, but I did find out that Emily had gone overnight to Ojai. The Cosmic Aid Foundation, I thought, and continued on to the Albergo Picasso.

Koontz was conferring with a couple of other detectives by a squad car in front of the hotel when I got there. One of them, a dark, skinny Chicano with a beaked Mayan nose, I took to be Estrada. Some comics I recognized from the Fun Zone were standing in a cluster a few feet away, watching and commenting like some weird Greek chorus of the entertainment-industry unemployed. I could almost hear their wisecracks about dead Romanians when I walked up to Koontz.

"How're you doin', Art?"

He pretended to ignore me, going over a dot matrix printout with the other detectives. I waited for them to leave before I addressed the inspector.

"What happened to Nastase?"

"Wine, is there any reason I should cooperate with you?"

He scowled at me, but I smiled back at him. This wasn't a time to get hostile. "I might help solve the crime."

"You might and you might not. You might actually create more problems than you solve. I understand you visited here last night, masquerading as the owner of some leather store. Pretty sleazy work you do.''

"Is lying a crime, Koontz?"

"I don't know. Ask your psychiatrist."

He looked at me with a sarcastic, knowing smirk. I did my best to ignore it and get back to business.

"How'd Nastase go?"

"You are persistent, aren't you?"

"It's a racial characteristic."

He took a deep breath. "All right. Look, your friend Nastase was found dead way in the back of the Tujunga Wash with a thirty-eight slug through his temple. The way he was hidden under the brush, I don't think whoever did it banked on his being found for a while. Who could've known some jerkoff William Morris agents get their rocks off up there three mornings a week playing war games with blank guns?"

"You still think it's drug-related?"

"Think? We know. You won't find this in the papers to-morrow, but we found an entire laboratory in the basement of Nastase's house this afternoon."

"Oh, yeah? Where's that?"

"LeMoyne Street in Echo Park."

"Thanks. You're a sweetheart."

"Put it down to sympathy for the victims of international terrorism. But remember, it'll only happen once. *And* you owe me."

"Absolutely."

He turned away and pushed through a group of comics into the hotel.

"How many Romanians does it take to change a light bulb?" one of them asked me.

"Not funny," I said and got into my car. I was already late for my private detective class at the Learning League.

School was held on the second-floor office level of a run-down stucco mini-mall in East Hollywood. The first floor was occupied by a Laundromat, a real estate office, and a liquor store. I resisted stopping at the liquor store for another lottery ticket and climbed the stairs to the second floor. The room was mostly filled when I entered and the class was already in progress. I shuffled around to the back and took a seat as if I belonged there. Chantal Barrault gave me a curious look from across the room and I smiled back at her, then directed my attention to the teacher. He was a short dark guy in his thirties with a mustache, wearing baggy pants and an olive warm-up jacket with epaulets and sleeves that zipped off. More trendiness. He had written his name, Peter Roman, on the blackboard with the number of his investigator's license. At the moment, since this was a *California* adult education class, he was going around the room asking the students what *they* did and why *they* wanted to take the class. The first three guys were television writers for *Simon & Simon* and were interested in background for their series. The next woman was a widow who liked to take courses. Then the next four—two guys and two women—were also television writers, this time for *Remington Steele. They* were looking for a story. The man next to them was a mystery writer. He was looking for authenticity for his books. There was no question: we were definitely in Los Angeles.

"I guess this is one of those times no one really wants to be a detective," Roman joked nervously.

Everybody looked relieved when they got around to Chantal and she said she was a stand-up comic who was "actually interested for real" in a career as a private investigator.

When they came around to me, I gave a fictitious name and said I was a process server who wanted to move up. Roman smiled in commiseration—someone was lower than he was—and began the class. I immediately did what I usually did in school—go to sleep. I remember vaguely hearing something about methods of obtaining information (public records, surveillance, pretext) and something about thinking like an investigator, whatever that was, and then it was break time. Roman had given the class an assignment—to locate the best vantage point for an auto surveillance of the mini-mall cleaners—and they were all running around the second-floor balcony with pencils and Xeroxed maps of the neighborhood. I thought it was all a load of nonsense. In reality, there were so many variables in a situation like that, there never could be one right answer. But Chantal was taking it very seriously. She was standing by the balcony rail, clutching her pencil and staring intently at the traffic patterns on Sunset Boulevard.

"Interested in some practical experience?" I said, walking up to her.

She didn't appear to hear me.

"The best car for surveillance is a van with a lot of windows. That way you can get up and walk around. Also, carry a goody bag with a cheap camera you're not afraid to toss over your shoulder, a pair of binoculars, *Thomas's Street Guide,* a few quick and dirty disguises, a flashlight, and an empty coffee can for peeing if you're a man. I don't know what you're going to do. Hold it in, I suppose. Also never do a rolling surveillance in a car with front end damage. It's a dead giveaway."

"What're you talking about?"

"I'm offering you a job, Chantal. If you want to be a private investigator, you can start tonight. Of course, you'll have to miss the second half of the class."

"Are you serious? . . . You *are* serious. Well, I, uh, let's go."

Two minutes later we were out on the street.

"Where's your car?" I asked.

"I don't have one."

"You don't have a *car?* In *Los Angeles?*"

"Listen, *mon ami,* you try making it as a stand-up comic in this town and see how long *you* keep *your* car."

"You haven't tried being a private detective yet. . . . All right, what the hell, we'll rent you one. Right now we've got a cushy client."

I opened the doors of the BMW. She got in on the passenger side.

"Look," she explained as we drove off, "I've done a lot of things in my life. You've just caught me at a bad time. But I hope you know what you're doing, because I don't like being a charity case. Even in my worst moments I've never done that. I didn't even take a penny of alimony from my ex-husband even though he could've afforded plenty."

"Who was he?"

"A psychiatrist."

I groaned.

"What's the matter? You have a problem with psychiatrists?"

"No, no. I'm just, uh, surrounded.... Okay, here's my proposition. For this case I'll pay you twelve dollars an hour plus expenses. Sometimes you'll be working with me. Sometimes alone. But any time there's shit work, it'll be for you to do."

"I don't go out for coffee. I promised myself whatever I did I'd rather be a bag woman than—"

"I'm not talking about that. I'm talking about grunt research. Going to the library, that kind of thing. Did you tell them at the Fun Zone that you were quitting stand-up?"

"What for? Why close off options? You never know. There could've been a scout from the Letterman show and—"

"Great. That's what I like to hear. Now, listen ..." I told her what I knew about the Ptak case, or most of it, about Emily and Otis and Nastase and Bannister. About Koontz and the suspected drug ring, even about the William Morris agents in Tujunga.

"So tonight," I concluded, "I'm going to have a look around Nastase's place. I want you to go down to the Fun Zone and see what you can find out. Maybe go over to the Albergo Picasso, too. They know me now, but you're just a nosy comic looking around like the rest of them. I'll meet you back at the club around midnight."

When I was done, she looked at me for what they used to call a long minute. "Why do you trust *me* with all this?" she said.

"Shouldn't I?"

"Well, yeah, sure, but"— she shrugged— "you don't exactly know me."

"I've got to trust someone. Besides, I have a great instinct for these things. I discovered my ex-wife was cheating on me in only *four years.*"

Chantal grinned as we pulled up at the rent-a-car office. We got out and I put a Datsun on my credit card for her and headed off for Echo Park. The odd thing was, by the time I crossed Western, I was starting to feel like I was missing her.

That changed to a feeling of unease the moment I drove onto LeMoyne Street. To begin with, I used to live in the Echo Park area and it always made me uncomfortable to return to old neighborhoods. I made a note to ask Nathanson about that. But more disturbing than the neighborhood was the street itself. It was poorly lit and sparsely populated, winding up erratically along an eroded ridge of smog-damaged eucalyptus and deteriorated twenties bungalows to die out in a concrete retaining wall whose faded mural of Quetzalcoatl was stained brown from a storm drain and webbed with cracks.

I parked near this wall and walked down half a block to an off-white bungalow surrounded with pampas grass. Some leftover yellow barricade tape with LAPD on the gate and on the front door identified it as Nastase's. No one appeared to be around. The lab squad had probably come and gone already, doing their number in their fire-retardant jump suits as they carried out the acetone and ether that was used to lace the coke. I hoped they had gotten it all, because one false step with that stuff could mean bye-bye to this street and a couple of adjoining canyons.

I checked the neighboring houses. One of them was abandoned and the other was about a hundred and fifty feet farther down the hill behind a row of spiny century plants. Then I walked around the back of Nastase's place, my feet crunching more loudly than I intended on the dead eucalyptus pods. The side of the house was boarded up and the rear had a small porch and a useless backyard that sloped off at a forty-degree angle into the gully below. The porch screens were ripped and the screen door hung loosely from a hinge. Where the earth had slipped away into the gully, I could see the foundations decomposing. This flimsy structure was a far cry from the block fortresses one had come to identify with cocaine laboratories, but then who knew? It was certainly isolated enough.

I climbed up on a crate and looked into the room next to the kitchen. It was a laundry made over into a laboratory, all right, and a pretty crude one at that. There were still some white plastic buckets hanging around, the kind you buy in any hardware store and which are often used to wash the coke paste. I could smell the odor of hydrochloric acid, the wash chemical, coming from the sink. In the opposite corner, by an old washer and dryer, were stacks of cardboard boxes that must not have had any evidentiary use because they were left behind by the police. The bottom four had the words "Holy Bible—Made in USA" printed on the side. I wanted a better look, so I reached up farther and found a break in the outer sash of the window, pulling it toward me while pushing on the jamb. The upper half of the window went crashing into the room, a couple of panes of glass shattering on the cement floor. I was about to hoist myself in when a piece of brick came flying past my head, rebounding off the broken screen.

"Hey, smart dog, what you doin' here?"

I looked around slowly to see a pair of Korean punkers in baggy suits and dark glasses staring at me. The one who spoke was fat and wore his hair orange and long. "You been tryin' to fuck with the Reverend, smart dog?" I didn't have a chance to answer before he continued, "Anybody fuckin' with the Reverend gotta deal with the Chu's Brothers." He and his partner started advancing on me. "We call ourselves the Chu's Brothers 'cause you get to choose between us." Orange hair laughed at his own joke. Then he stopped five feet in front of me, right alongside his blue-haired partner. Simultaneously they pulled out a chain and a pair of *nunchako* sticks. "So choose."

I thought of what the teachers at Simon's *hapkido* studio could do with those sticks and it didn't take me long to decide. I jumped as high and hard as I could between them. But the Chu's Brothers were one step ahead of me. They had already chosen.

8 The first person I saw when I came to was Chantal.

"Is this lesson one?" she asked. "Or were you just standing me up? I was waiting in front of the Fun Zone for an hour and a half. Thank God, you've got a good excuse."

I would've slammed her if I could've moved.

"Just be still and do what I say. I used to work in an emergency room."

"I know. I know. You used to do everything." I groaned, but I did as she said, rolling gingerly over onto my side so she could see which and how many of my ribs were cracked. My guess was about a hundred. If this was how I felt after duking it out with a couple of Korean pogo freaks, one thing was certain—I'd never be Rambo.

"You'll be all right," she said. "Come on. We'd better get you out of here."

I started struggling to my feet. "How'd you—?"

"You said you'd be at Nastase's and it's three A.M. You think I'd let my partner rot in some canyon to be eaten by the coyotes?"

"Your *partner?* Aren't we being a little hasty here?"

"Well, you know. It's a manner of speaking."

"Une façon de parler."

"Where'd you learn *that?*"

"High school. But don't test me."

"I think that's very nice. You know a little French."

"Oh, fuck you."

We ... or rather I stumbled up to the top of the ridge and followed Chantal uncomplainingly to the Datsun. It was parked about fifty yards from Nastase's place and I glanced over at the house. All was silent. The Chu's Brothers seemed to have gone, but in my present condition I didn't have a strong inclination to find out for sure.

"These Korean punks," said Chantal as we drove off down the hill. "What were they after?"

"I don't know," I said. Right then I had visions of them yanking the Blaupunkt out of the dash of my BMW. It would've been the fourth one. But what the hell? I was making my own small contribution to stabilizing the price of car radios. "Maybe it was some free coke gear, but the police already got most of that. The way they laid into me, Angel Dust looked more their thing anyway ... unless they were traveling Bible salesmen."

"I thought I was supposed to be the comedian."

"No joke. There were four cartons of Bibles sitting in the corner of the lab."

"That's pretty strange for a drug dealer."

"Yeah. And on top of that they were laying on some bullshit about some reverend."

"You know something else strange—Nastase went to Trieste every three months."

"On a bellhop's salary? How'd you find that out?"

"The elevator operator at the Albergo Picasso. He's a

Greek. They go fishing together every Sunday off Cabrillo Beach."

"Good luck," I said. "The fish down there are dead before you catch 'em." Then I clutched my side. The pain transmitters around my rib cage were suddenly making a frontal assault on my nervous system.

"Here," said Chantal, reaching into her purse for a tightly rolled joint. "This should help."

"Thanks," I said.

I tried to suck on it, but the pain was so severe, my lungs weren't letting anything in. I didn't start to feel better until we got to emergency at Queen of Angels, where they gave me a couple of Percodans, X-rayed me, and taped my sides. The X ray showed one broken rib and a mass of bruises. The cause of accident was listed as "fall." By then the Percodans were working pretty well.

I woke up late the next morning to the sound of someone unlocking my apartment. I jumped out of bed, immediately wrenching the right side of my body with an unbelievable pain, grabbed a robe, and went into the living area. Chantal was heading into the kitchen with a bag of groceries.

"Good morning," she said, pulling out a carton of eggs, cheese, croissants, and coffee. "Do you like omelet gruyère à la Mère Poulard?"

"A la Mère Who? ... Sure.... You didn't have to do this, you know. It doesn't come with the job description."

"No problem." She broke some eggs into a bowl and began beating them with a whisk. "By the way, this twelve dollars an hour you're paying me, when does it begin and end?"

"We'll have to talk about that." She poured the eggs deftly into a sizzling pan, swirling it back and forth the way I had seen Julia Child do it on television. "You're very good at this. You know, no woman's *really* made me breakfast since my ex-wife joined a consciousness-raising group in 1971. Usually they suggest we go out to Duke's or something." I looked at her. She was wearing tight-fitting jeans and a white T-shirt that said VIVE LE QUÉBEC LIBRE on the back. "The first Mr. Chantal, the shrink, was pretty lucky. What happened to him, anyway?"

"I wasn't ready to settle down, but he was. I didn't have the courage to tell him, so I started fooling around with other guys. Soon . . ." She shrugged and slid the omelet onto a plate. Then she added a couple of croissants and carried them out to me at the dining table. "You work out of your home?"

"It's cheaper that way."

"Did you ever think it presents a less than professional image?"

"Yeah. I've been thinking of moving out . . . starting an agency . . . but I'm waiting."

"For what?"

"I don't know. A lottery win." I didn't know how to answer better than that and I was grateful when I was interrupted, almost immediately, by the phone. I picked up. It was Bannister and he sounded upset.

"Mr. Wine . . . uh, Moses, I mean . . . I hate doing this on the phone, but I've got an emergency on my hands."

I glanced up at Chantal, who was pouring some coffee.

"It's the Grand Shrink," I said, cupping the phone in one hand while stabbing a piece of omelet.

"Are you alone?"

"Enough."

"What do you mean 'enough'? Can I be direct with you?"

"You're a psychiatrist. You're supposed to be."

"Don't be cute with me, Wine. This could be a calamity."

"Go ahead."

"Yes, well, uh, Otis disappeared last night. He got up when he and my son were watching a tape of *Terminator* and never came back."

"How'd he get out?"

"He took the louvers out of the jalousie window in the bathroom. He must've gone straight across the tennis court to the Coast Highway. I have reason to believe he took the red-eye to New York."

"How do you know that?"

"He told my son some mysterious person called him in the middle of the night to say his brother was in grave danger."

"Do you believe him?"

"I don't know. Otis is capable of making up anything if it'll give him an excuse to get near the powder. My son wasn't sure either. He said Otis was acting pretty crazy."

"Where were you at the time?"

"Attending to another patient. I can't be six people. . . . Moses, I'd like to hire you to go find him. It's very important that he be back as soon as possible, both for his own protection and because it would be disastrous for his career if the studio found out he was gone."

"Not to mention yours."

"Yes, mine too." There was a pregnant pause. I looked over at Chantal again. She was watching me with the same intensity with which she had studied the Xerox sheet at the private eye course. I realized this woman could learn all she needed to know about being a detective in about four days. I also realized my omelet was getting cold and swallowed another bite. "This has to be done right away, Moses. By Saturday." Bannister interpreted my silence as acquiescence.

"Why Saturday?"

"Because Otis is scheduled to be master of ceremonies for the Comedians and Chefs Benefit for Africa at Matthew Rodman's mansion in Bel Air. The whole entertainment community will be there."

"Comedians and *chefs?*"

"Yes. You know, chefs—Wolfgang Puck of Spago, that Waters woman up in Berkeley. They're the biggest thing going today. And now Sandor Romulus of Bistro Vegas—he's catering the affair. And for obvious reasons they wanted the hottest young *black* comic to headline the show. They've already sold five hundred tickets at a hundred and twenty-five apiece. Most of the major studios are buying blocks."

"Look, Doctor, I'd like to help you. But as you know, I'm working for Emily Ptak and there might be a conflict of int—"

"Don't worry. I've already talked to Emily about this. Besides, she's one of the sponsors of the benefit. It's important for her, too."

"The Cosmic Aid Foundation."

"Right. We've agreed to handle all your expenses in New York, of course. I suggest you get on the next convenient flight."

"So I'm to be working for you now, as well as for Emily."

"No, no. You'd still be working for Emily primarily. There'd just be this one overlap."

I told him I'd call him back in a few minutes and hung up. I needed to think this over. I shoveled in a forkful more omelet while Chantal waited impatiently for me to fill her in on what was happening.

"So we're going to New York," she said before I had barely finished my explanation.

"Not you, me. And not New York, the Bronx. If I don't miss my guess, that's where Otis'll be hanging out. It's a waste of money for two of us to go."

"No problem. I have friends in the Bronx. Montrealers who wanted to open a *pâtisserie* on the Grand Concourse until they realized it was a Puerto Rican neighborhood. Now they run a laundry. I could stay with them."

"It's still a waste of money."

"I'll fly People's. I don't mind arriving in Newark. It's easier than—"

"And I don't want to have to worry about you in the Bronx, unless, among your other undiscovered talents, you're a fifth-degree black belt in something or other."

"And I suppose in *your* condition you're ready to deal with—"

"*I'll* be the judge of that. Now, as far as I know, you're working for me and I need you to stay here." Chantal was starting to look pissed. I recognized the symptoms from long experience and I moved on quickly before I was accused of sexism. "For one thing, I'm waiting to hear from an aging shamus named Stanley Burckhardt about a post office box in Glendale. I want you to stay on top of that. I'll give you the details. Also, I'd like you to go out to Malibu and keep your eyes on the comings and goings at Carl Bannister's shrinkery. Let me know if you find out anything interesting." I figured that last would mollify her for the moment.

"What about the Chu's Brothers?"

"I'll call a friend on the LAPD Asian Squad and see if they have anything. You can follow up on that. And rent all the video cassettes you can find of Mike Ptak. I doubt they'll tell us much, but you never know. Also stay tuned for further developments at the Fun Zone and keep in touch with your Greek elevator operator at the Picasso. That sounds like a full calendar, doesn't it?"

"I love New York," she said forlornly.

"We're not operating a travel agency here. And as far as I'm concerned, your meter's running forty hours a week at twelve dollars per. That makes four hundred and eighty dollars weekly. You can add reasonable expenses to that. But don't go overboard. I don't think Emily Ptak would like you taking elevator operators to Spago, even if she does. Save your receipts."

And with that I finished my omelet, picked up the phone, and made my calls: Emily, who verified what Bannister had told me and said she had no idea why Otis called her a "mind-fucking cunt" other than because he was paranoid and hated all white people uncontrollably "when it suited his purposes"; John Lu with the Asian Squad, who wasn't in (I left Chantal's number); Nathanson's service, to say I'd be missing my next appointment; and, finally, Bannister again.

"Any idea where I should look?" I asked.

"He has a girl friend named Della who lives in one of the projects."

"What's her second name?"

"I don't know. He always just called her Della. She's half Puerto Rican and has a three-year-old kid. But she told him she wouldn't see him until he kicked coke. That freaked him out. Then there's his manager, a real dumbbell lawyer named Purvis Wilkes who has an office near Yankee Stadium. Otis is absurdly loyal to him. And, of course, his brother, King."

"King?"

"King King."

"Where do I find him?"

"No idea. But if you do, I'm sure the DEA would like to know. From what I hear he controls half the drug trade for the South Bronx."

9 I got out of the gypsy cab on the Grand Concourse with a strong sense of déjà vu. I hadn't been in this neighborhood very often since I was a little boy and went to Yankee games with my father. The area had gone through several changes since then, down to the bottom and halfway back again, but it was the earlier period of my childhood that was on my mind as I crossed the street to Purvis Wilkes's office, passing a deli that had been Jewish, Puerto Rican, and was now some weird mixture of Latino and Arabic, serving, I imagined, chorizos on pita with canned piña coladas and Turkish delight for dessert. The place I had gone to before the games for pastrami sandwiches with my father had disappeared, replaced by an Off-Track Betting parlor. Not that we would go there that often. Usually we went to the Stadium Club because my father and his lawyer friends, season ticket holders, were members and that was what a man did, had a steak lunch at the Stadium Club and then sat in a box on the third base line, while his son stared with a combination of curiosity and envy at the black and brown people in the bleachers.

There was nothing Wall Street about Purvis Wilkes's office. Actually, it was more reminiscent of a credit dentist, nestled like a bomb shelter into the dirty-yellow brick courtyard of one of those soot-ridden Concourse apartment buildings in which all the first-floor windows are honeycombed with steel grid antitheft wire. Wilkes's window looked as if it had been smashed a few times anyway. The name on the door read Feinstein & Wilkes, Attorneys at Law, but Feinstein, I later found out, had defrauded a couple of clients and skipped for Minneapolis some time ago, ending this supposedly ecumenical partnership.

Wilkes himself was a tall, slightly paunchy man in his early thirties with light sepia skin and a neatly cut Vandyke. He was reading the paper and listening to an old Thelonious Monk album on the radio when his secretary introduced me. The way he acted, he didn't seem overeager for clients. He seemed even less eager when I told him what I wanted.

"Hey, I'm Otis's manager. If I told some private dick where he was, think how long I'd have that job."

"But as Otis's manager you should have his best interests at heart. The show business community is one tiny hornet's nest of gossip. Word gets out Otis went bye-bye and you can say sayonara to the fat movie contract. The people out there are getting supersensitive to drug publicity."

"Oh, yeah? Who're they afraid of? Nancy Reagan?"

I half smiled.

"Anyway, we got a contract, so what's the big deal? Listen, you look like a decent guy." Wilkes leaned back and lit up a Jamaican cigar. "Jewish intellectual ... guilty ... smart. One of those ex-civil-rights dudes gone confused because the brothers have rejected you. You oughtta be ashamed of yourself, workin' for that social-climbing Svengali Bannister. That sinister fuck'll do anything to get his claws into Otis. You call that therapy? Filling Otis's head with all kinds of vile shit over a little toot?"

"More than a little toot, if word has it correctly."

"All right. More than a little. But so what? He's not hurting anybody except for himself. And Bannister's shameless. He even tried to get to be Otis's beneficiary. Can you believe that? ... Janelle, where are you, girl? Bring this man some coffee."

Janelle sashayed into the room with the coffeepot, five foot six of exquisitely formed burnt siena flesh bursting out of a beige silk paratrooper jump suit. This was the kind of black woman that would normally start my blood percolating so fast I'd have steam coming out of my ears in under thirty seconds, but this time, oddly, I scarcely reacted. I hadn't reacted on the plane either when the stewardess practically grabbed my crotch while pouring me a Bloody Mary. I wondered why that was and the image of Chantal filtered up through my brain like a holograph. I pushed it away and focused on Wilkes.

"I share your opinion of Bannister, Purvis. But I'm not really working for him. I'm working for Emily. Ptak's widow."

"Sister Salvation? You gotta be kidding. What's she after? There's not enough famine in Africa, she gotta be sending you to the Bronx?"

"What she's after is trying to figure out why her husband committed suicide. More important to you is that the L.A. police think it had something to do with some massive drug connection between Hollywood and the Bronx."

Wilkes broke up laughing. "That's pretty funny, isn't it?"

"My guess is Otis thought they were going to connect him into it. That's why he split. Apparently, in the middle of the night, some mysterious person called him to warn him his brother was in trouble."

Suddenly Wilkes wasn't laughing. He waved Janelle out of the room with the back of his hand.

"King's too smart for shit like that," he said. "He's a businessman. He doesn't intrude on the province of other businessmen."

"Where is King?"

"You never know."

"What about Otis?"

Wilkes stared at me. "You know, a boy like you could get killed fucking around where you don't belong."

"Couple of people already *have* been killed—Mike Ptak and a Romanian named Nastase."

"And what do you expect me to do about that? Let me tell you something about the way the world works around here, my white liberal friend. Otis King's mother was a hooker who died of an overdose when he was four years old. His father's doing ten-to-twenty at Riker's Island for knifing a man in the back. Otis himself was out on the street by the time he was nine. Got his first robbery conviction at eleven and spent the years twelve to fifteen in juvenile hall. If he couldn't make people laugh, he'd be spending most of his life in jail for sure. Because it would have been the *only way* he could've survived. Only way he could eat, because the motherfucker can't read, can't spell. He can barely count to twenty. He's no different from the rest of those assholes out on the street there spending their days shooting China white because it's the only way they can make it till dark without killing themselves. That's the way it is here, Mr. Wine. And that's the way it's always been. And if you think people from *my* world are ripping off *your* world, you gotta be crazy. It's the other way around! Now, get out!''

I stumbled out of Wilkes's office wondering what I had done to deserve this. I was tired of black people holding me responsible for everything from food stamp cutbacks to the Zionist conspiracy. And I was tired of excusing myself for things I had about as much to do with as the last space walk. I was about to go back in and give him a piece of it when Janelle came running out on the sidewalk straight up to me. "Hey, wait! Wait a minute, Mr. Wine ... Otis needs help. He's gonna die out there on those streets if he stays any longer ... like one of those zoo animals they send back and they can't live in the jungle anymore.''

"I know what you mean," I said.

She looked at me a moment, trying to decide whether she could trust me or not. "You know Della?''

"You mean Otis's girl friend?''

"Yeah. She said she was with him last night, but she kicked him out because he was so loaded.''

"Any idea where he went?''

"Maybe. She didn't say.''

"Where does Della live?''

"Oh, hey, you don't wanna go there. That's not a smart place to go.''

"I know it's not smart, but where is it?''

She looked back at the building. Wilkes was standing in his office window.

"I gotta go."

She started off, but I grabbed her by the arm.

"Tremont Avenue Projects, number Seventeen B. But don't go in by 179th Street."

"I won't," I said, letting her go. She ran back into the building before I could say thanks.

It took me about twenty minutes to find a cab that would take me up to the Tremont Avenue Projects. But when I got there, I was surprised to find it wasn't half as bad as I expected. A few junkies were wandering down 179th Street in the midday sun that late October afternoon, but there was nothing particularly threatening about the neighborhood with its variety stores, hardware shops, and paint outlets. Some of the streets were cobblestoned and there was even a quaint reminder of the old Bronx in the way the road meandered up the hill toward Van Cortlandt Park.

The project itself was in remarkably good shape for public housing dedicated, according to the bronze plaque, in 1962 by then Bronx Borough President Joseph Periconi. Only a handful of windows were broken and most of the graffiti had been restricted to the handball courts, the recognized canvas for the art form. Even the lawns were relatively clean, with a few flower beds sprinkled here and there.

Just beyond the courts and over a chain link fence a group of aspiring Dr. Js were visible, practicing their slams and jams in bright orange and black uniforms that said Tremont Avenue Dunk Club. I stood there watching them a moment, wondering what politician was reaping what benefit keeping this particular housing project in such classy shape, when a Rolls-Royce Silver Cloud drove past me and slowed by the

Dunk Club, three brand-new basketballs flying out of the Rolls's window and over the fence into the hands of the club members, who cheered and waved as the Rolls drove off.

I looked from them over to the forbidden 179th Street entrance. A couple of junkies were weaving between the two seven-story buildings past a baby in a carriage, but nothing seemed particularly ominous until my gaze drifted up to the tops of the buildings where, on each side, two men in berets oddly reminiscent of the old Black Panthers were standing on opposite roofs surveying the area. They each held walkie-talkies and crossed back and forth along the roof's edge in paramilitary fashion. Before they noticed me, I turned and headed around the block, moving at the pace of the average Bronx pedestrian, which meant fast enough to avoid trouble but not too fast to attract attention. In five minutes I came around the other side of the project on Knox Avenue. The street was narrower there and I stayed close to the building to avoid surveillance. Nothing had happened, yet I felt a tingling, urgent sensation on the edge of paranoia. I kept my eyes straight ahead and moved with the purposefulness of someone who knew where he was going. By the time I reached the rear entrance to the project, my hands were damp and I was feeling a little light-headed. I made a quick right through a gate and came through the entrance where two of the buildings formed a cul-de-sac. I walked straight through the nearest door into a stairwell. A couple of dozen men, most of them looking pretty stoned, were lined up on the stairs, shuffling about and talking to themselves as if they were waiting for a store to open. They stared at me blankly as some guy came lurching down the stairs, clutching a small balloon. I was about to turn and leave, when, from out of nowhere, someone grabbed my arm. It was one of the watchmen in the black berets. When I looked at him, I saw he was sixteen, maybe seventeen, just the age of my older son. He grabbed the sleeve of my jacket and yanked it upward, revealing what appeared then to be a very pale white inner arm clearly devoid of tracks.

"What're you doing here?" he said.

"I'm looking for Seventeen B."

"Oh, yeah. Well, you got the wrong building. You're lying to me. You're a narc, motherfucker!"

"I'm not a narc. I'm looking for a girl in Seventeen B."

"Sniffin' poontang, Charlie?" someone shouted.

Everyone started to laugh. I began to back out of the building as quickly as I could, but I hadn't gotten five feet when two more guys, both about the size of New York Jets linemen and both wearing the obligatory berets, were at my side, lifting me off the ground as they escorted me out the door, through the gate, and into the backseat of the same Silver Cloud I had seen, moments before, dispensing basketballs like the lead vehicle in a drug dealer's antipoverty program.

10

"Do you like Eastern seafood, Mr. Wine? The scrod is good. I particularly recommend the scrod this time of year." He pronounced it "scrahd" like a proper Bostonian.

"Fine. I'll take the scrod."

"Two scrod, Eddie," he told the waiter. "Lightly grilled with lemon. And bring us a side order of your cottage fries. I feel like going off my diet today."

Eddie nodded and slipped off. I was sitting opposite King King in Nick's Sea Grotto on City Island, a minute enclave of the middle-class good life floating incongruously off the eastern shore of the Bronx. Through the window to my right was a tiny marina, a pier, and some rustic Cape Cod frame houses. It could have been Falmouth or Hyannis. King himself fit in perfectly, the well-groomed but casual professional in a pale green Fila jogging suit, Sperry Top-Siders, and a beeper on his belt. Even the car was right, a 1985 black Jeep Cherokee with wood siding and fog lamps. He was waiting by it when the Silver Cloud pulled up to deposit me. He signaled its drivers on with a dismissive wave of the hand meant to indicate, incontestably, that parading around in a vehicle like that was a sign of unspeakable vulgarity.

"I had an interesting fish on my last visit to California," said King. "Orange roughy. From New Zealand."

"You get out West often, Mr. King?"

"Hardly ever. I don't like the weather. Too consistent. And the real estate prices are a joke." He sipped on his beer. "Though I understand some people think I have great interests out there."

"Some people do. But you seem to be doing pretty well where you are. Your business looks about as well organized as General Motors."

"Things aren't what they appear to be, Mr. Wine. And I can assure you I suffer from the same syndromes as other businessmen. Too many people on the payroll, murderous competition, and the IRS snooping around every little nook and cranny. They don't realize that if they put me out of business, the city has massive unemployment all the way from 149th Street to the Cross Bronx Expressway. But the fact is, right now I'd do anything to get out of it."

"Come on now, King. You don't look like a man who's struggling to stay afloat."

"It's not that simple." His beeper sounded and he switched it off. "Do you have any children, Mr. Wine?"

"Two boys."

"Lucky man. I'd do anything to have children. Move to Detroit. Have a house in Grosse Pointe. But I have to get out of this business first."

"So get out."

"It's the only thing I know. I've been doing it since Otis and I were kids. I was six years old when I sold my first nickel bag to one of the fifth-graders in my grammar school. But I *am* going to get out," he said, "and I'm going to get out big.... See this?" He took out a small notebook and dropped it on the table. "My vocabulary list. Every time someone uses a big word, I write it down here and look it up when I get home: euphemism . . . perspicacious." He read a couple from the top. "Soon I'll be ready to make every one of those white-bread fucks at the Harvard Club look sick. I'll take my rightful place as King King, captain of industry . . . as soon as I get my stake."

"Your stake?"

"I want to buy in on a level commensurate with my position. Wouldn't you, Mr. Wine? After all, here in the Bronx I have a certain status and, I'm sure you would agree, the skills it takes to run my business are not altogether different from those it takes to run a conglomerate."

I looked at King. On one level he was a delusional, vicious, dope-dealing bastard, but on another he made perfect sense.

"Where does Otis fit in all this?"

"Otis is crazy. He's all emotion and can't hold anything in. When there's a threat on my life, he's absolutely out of control. He thinks he's helping me, but he's hurting me. Lots of people would be interested in getting the feds on my path, take over my business. I'm a moving target and Otis is a liability because he's so visible. Makes him guilty. You know what I mean. So he comes here, he doesn't even see me. And then when Della shines him on, he's gone. God knows where he is." Our scrod arrived and King started in on it immediately. "He was better off when Ptak was around. He kept him on the ground. Of course, their partnership was doomed anyway."

"Because Ptak didn't have the talent."

"Oh, yeah, everybody knew that. Even Ptak. But he didn't

want to be in show business anyway. He was the one who broke the partnership with Otis."

"He did?"

King looked at me suspiciously. "You didn't know that?"

"All the Hollywood press reported it the other way around."

"Well, sure, what're they gonna say? But Ptak had other plans."

"What kind of plans?"

"What do you want to know that for?"

"I'm investigating. It's my job."

"Some job." He laughed softly. "Eat your scrod."

I ate my scrod. Then I said, "For a guy who wants to have children and move to Grosse Pointe, you're pretty cavalier about this LAPD investigation."

"What're you trying to do, gumshoe, put some muscle on me? Make me tell you some secret that's going to unlock your case? Let me tell you, there's no kind of muscle you can put on me. You're a slimy little private eye and I'm a major businessman. I make more money in a day than you make in a year."

"I wouldn't doubt it."

"And Mike Ptak needed me more than I needed him."

"What would he need from you?" I added a little smirk to the end of my question because I figured it might make him defensive. It did.

"My expertise."

"Don't tell me Mike Ptak wanted to go into your kind of business."

"How stupid can you be? No wonder you're a cheap gumshoe."

"So Ptak wanted to go into legitimate business."

"Investment banking."

"And what did he have to offer the world of investment banking?"

"Nothing. He just suffered from what you might call an inflated self-image."

"What do you mean?"

"Well, I'll tell you, Mr. Investigator, because it doesn't matter now anyway. The man's history. He said he knew how to put his hands on twenty-five million dollars." King grinned at me. "Now I bet you're thinking, Where can I get hold of this twenty-five million dollars?"

"Very good guess."

"I told you I was a business genius." He grinned again, then sat there a moment enjoying the silence. "Well, don't waste your time with that, because I can assure you I checked it out fully and Ptak's twenty-five mil was a stone fantasy."

"Checked it out with whom?"

"Figure that out for yourself. Besides, that would've been *real* dirty money. Scum money. So dirty even *I* wouldn't touch it." He checked his watch and frowned. "Now I've talked so long I won't be able to finish my lunch." King stood and put his initials on the back of the check. "This one's on me. But for your own health, stay away from housing projects in the Bronx. It's not Seventy-seven Sunset Strip, if you know what I mean. And one other thing—if someone's trying to nail my ass for this Ptak business, there's a good chance, since you're poking around in my affairs, they might want to take a crack at you and blame *me* for it. It's the kind of headline they love in the *New York Post:* 'L.A. Private Dick Blown Away by Black Drug Lord.' Or maybe they'd just dump you off a pier and leave you there. You wouldn't want to end up one of those bloated corpses found every so often floating along with the garbage in the Harlem River, now would you?''

"I'll ruminate on that."

"Ru-what? What'd you say?" he asked, pulling out his little notebook. I spelled it for him. "Thanks," said King and left, leaving me sitting there with the scrod.

I stared at it for a second, wondering what kind of money was so dirty even King King wouldn't touch it. When I didn't get anywhere with that, I returned to the problem at hand: finding Otis. Getting to him through Della didn't seem a particularly promising idea, given the welcome I was receiving at the Tremont Avenue Projects. And being a smart guy and trying to sneak back there by disguise or by some other trick of tradecraft was about as quick a route to ending my ambivalence about being a detective as I could think of. In fact, in all probability it would end whatever ambivalence I had about life. Then I thought of someone Otis had mentioned during our laid-back California lunch at the Malibu Pharmacy. It was a flimsy lead indeed, but for the moment it was all I had.

Before I acted upon it, I went over to the restaurant pay phone and dialed home to see what was happening. It had been a late lunch and a good portion of the day would have passed on the West Coast. An answering machine picked up and I thought I had the wrong number until I realized Chantal had recorded a new message in a cool, professional tone:

"You have reached the offices of Moses Wine International Investigative Consultants, specializing worldwide in missing persons, technical surveillance, industrial espionage, witness analysis, domestic relations, personal injury, and related areas. All our operatives are engaged in field work at this time. If you leave a message, together with your name, number, and time you called, our staff will contact you as soon as possible."

Jesus, I thought, where did she get that jargon, the *Yellow Pages?*

I hung up and headed for the door of the restaurant, stopping by the cashier to find out where I could get the subway. It turned out I had to get a bus off the island and pick up the IND near Route 295, but all this complicated maneuvering stopped the moment I exited the restaurant and noticed a van parked across the street. It was a brand-new bronze Toyota without license plates and its driver was a tall, muscular white man with chestnut brown hair and an angular, chiseled face resembling the actor Scott Glenn—a killer's face. He was pretending not to look at me, but I could see that the sideview mirror of his van had been skewed slightly toward the front of the restaurant. King's warning about the Harlem River flashed through my mind and I quickly retreated inside. Ten seconds later the van drove off.

But it hadn't gone far because ten minutes later I caught it in the rearview mirror as I rode yet another gypsy cab west across the City Island Bridge back into the Bronx proper. My driver, Fouad Fayed, a Lebanese on a green card studying to be a civil engineer, was regaling me about the political significance of evenhandedness.

"It not evenhanded. It not evenhanded," he repeated about six times. "Don't take me amiss, but when the Arab man blow up in his office in Orange County, nobody care. But when the Jewish man, the old Jewish man in the wheelchair, about to die and everything, goes boom off that boat, everybody scream and yell like he Albert Schweitzer or something. Don't take me amiss."

"Don't take me amiss either, but see that bronze Toyota van right behind us?"

"I see. Yes. Good van. Japanese van. I for free trade, but we better have restrictions for that. Otherwise who buy American car? All industry go belly up. Green card worker first to go. Don't take me amiss."

"No chance of that. Look, why don't you drive a little faster?"

"Hey, mister, speed limit here twenty-five miles per hour."

"So what? Nobody's going to bother you. I'll pay the ticket." At that point we were heading east on 184th Street, the van a couple of car lengths behind us.

"I don't care ticket. Big deal ticket. But insurance go up. Big price. In this country, everybody sue, sue, sue."

"Okay, now listen to me and don't get nervous."

"I don't think I like what I going to hear."

"That car is following me."

"What for? Don't tell me. I don't want to know. Get out of my cab. No, don't get out. I won't stop. I die. Hold on." And he stepped on it.

In a moment we were hurtling between an oil truck and an abandoned school bus, the van barreling along behind us. We came out on the next street, both vehicles zigzagging through traffic, maintaining their distance until Fouad, his neck straining, floored the accelerator, jumped ahead, and made a hard right into a warehouse alley, getting a fifty-yard advantage on our pursuer.

"Where'd you learn to do that?"

"Drive ambulance for Beirut Red Cross."

"Pull in there." I pointed to a driveway. Fouad tucked in just as the van went whistling past. "Follow him."

"What're you, crazy? I no follow him. You get out of cab. Pay twelve dollars forty-five cents." He nodded toward his meter.

"Hey, listen, you're not going to abandon me now. We're old friends."

"Friend? I no friend of yours. I leave here right now. Have class Long Island University. Must study reserve book room. Otherwise fail. Good-bye." He leaned over the front seat, opening my door and muttering to himself.

"All right. Listen. Just drive me downtown like I asked you in the first place."

He looked at me, then, continuing to mutter, closed the door and drove off. In a few minutes we were crossing the Willis Avenue Bridge, Fouad watching me all the while in the rearview mirror, not saying a word. He finally spoke when we hit the FDR south.

"Mister, how come that man following you? Don't take me amiss."

"I think he wants to kill me."

"Oh, boy. Oh, boy. You the good guy or the bad guy? No, don't tell me."

"Okay, I won't."

He fell silent again until we reached Washington Square Park. "Okay, mister. Good-bye. I go."

"Hold on a second, Fouad. I'm not sure this is where I want to be."

"What you mean this not where you want to be? This Washington Square Park. What you talking?"

"I'm not sure my man is here."

"Look," he pointed. "Many men here. All kinds men. Women too. Faggots too. See how they dress up. Tomorrow Halloween. Big holiday for faggots. In my country everybody a faggot. No big deal. Men hold hands, but nobody gets cancer in the blood. No, no, no. They all die too young for that."

"I'm looking for some guy who might help me find another guy. What I'd like you to do is stay here." We were double-parked on the corner of Fourth and Macdougal. "Keep your meter running. I'll be right back. This is on account." I handed him a crisp fifty and got out of the cab. Emily's tab was mounting up.

In a few seconds I was wending my way through the action in the park. It was only six P.M., but the area was already jumping with the flotsam and jetsam of thirty years of American culture. Every fad since the war was represented and I wasn't sure which war. A toothless Jack Kerouac was sitting on a bench next to an earth mother who looked like she was still raising money for the Lincoln Brigade. Behind them a group of bisexual eleven-year-old punkers wearing their pre-Halloween masks were taunting an inept mime who was trying to climb the inevitable imaginary stairs. Over to their right, past some skateboarders and this year's Hare Krishnas, the crowds were gathering around Washington Square Fountain, small groups clustered about some eager beaver selling an inflation-diminished nickel bag or the latest psychedelic. It all reminded me of when I was a kid and would take the train down from Cos Cob to hear poetry readings at Rick's Café Bizarre. And I was mildly comforted that in their desperation to be new some things never changed.

I didn't see any comics among the street entertainers vying for an audience that evening, but I did notice a jazz musician playing some complicated fusion version of "Salt Peanuts" on a white plastic alto of the kind Ornette Coleman used to play, or, for all I knew, still did. I wandered over and joined the group of a dozen or so listening to him, waiting for him to finish the number. Despite a few days' growth and a faraway bloodshot look in his eyes, he still seemed to be in his late thirties. He wore a frayed hound's-tooth overcoat that swayed back and forth as he moved his sax to the beat of the music and a porkpie hat cocked sideways in the Lester Young style. He took it off when the song was over and started passing it around.

"How long you been playing around here?" I asked when he reached me.

"Too long."

"Swami X?" I said, depositing a twenty-dollar bill on top of the paltry collection of dimes and quarters he would take home for supper. It was strange to think that in his own weird way this guy was just as gifted a musician as Sting or David Byrne. But whoever said the world was fair?

"Swami X . . . Swami X." He looked at me. "Haven't seen

that dude in five years. Can't do comedy anymore because of his legs. Can't do stand-up when all you can do is sit down.''

''What happened to his legs?''

''Some Haitian junkie broke 'em with a baseball bat in Alphabet City. Got maybe fifteen dollars for his trouble. Not that it was a lot of trouble.''

''You know where he is now?''

''What're you gonna do when you find him?''

''Ask some questions.''

''Anybody gonna get hurt? Motherfucker's had enough problems, you know. There ain't a lot of jazz lovers left in this park, but twenty bucks don't buy my soul yet.'' He picked up his sax and played a few bars of a bebop version of the *Grosse Fugue*.

''He's not going to get hurt. At least by me.''

''There's a place called Shannon's Bar on Vesey Street in TriBeCa. Try the apartments upstairs.''

I got back into the cab, startling Fouad, who was gesturing with his fingers to a couple of punkettes on the corner of University Place as if they were a pair of stray cats.

''Vesey Street in TriBeCa.''

''Okay, okay. TriBeCa.'' He turned on the ignition and took off. I decided it was better not to mention the Toyota van, which suddenly pulled out about a half block behind us without its lights on. I wondered what kind of arsenal its driver kept in the recesses of his cabin. If he was as much of a professional as he looked, it was likely to be one of the newer weapons you read about in *Soldier of Fortune* magazine, like the Austrian 308-caliber Steyr rifle. With a good starlight scope, the kind they used in Vietnam to spot elusive VC on dark jungle nights, that sucker could hit a warthog at four hundred meters. And I was about twenty-five times bigger than a warthog.

We drove down Lower Broadway toward City Hall. I was starting to sweat. Maybe this wasn't such a good idea. Maybe I was endangering poor Fouad, who would have been better off at the L.I.U. reserve book room dealing with his civil engineering. By the time we reached Canal Street, I was convinced of it.

"Look, pull over," I said.

"What for, mister? You worried about man in van?" He gestured behind him. "I see him all the time at park. Never looks at girls. Don't take it amiss, but you are too nervous. He is bad guy. You good guy. Not to worry. Allah will punish him." And with that he made a hard left off of Canal and then a right down an alley. Then two more rights and a left. Then another alley and another right. I was in the hands of Allah.

By the time we hit Vesey Street the van was out of sight. "Over there," I said, pointing at Shannon's Bar, a dimly lit local joint with a shamrock in the window and a couple of missing letters in its neon sign. Fouad stopped out front.

"Keep circling the block," I said.

"Sure thing, mister," he replied. "Meter running."

"Yeah, right. Meter running."

Fouad disappeared, and I glanced in each direction past a row of decaying brick and cast-iron facades before entering the door immediately to the right of the bar, number 408.

The inside of the building was one of those older, dingy,

turn-of-the-century warehouses that cried out for gentrification but hadn't yet made it. The entryway was an ugly sea-green lit by a single bulb that revealed the name of the one-time residents: S & J IMPORTERS. It must have been a long time ago. There were several names on the building register, but none of them faintly resembled "Swami X." I had started up the stairs when a ferretlike character darted out at the top of the landing, his eyes bulging with urban paranoia.

"What do you want?" he said.

"Swami X. I'm looking for someone named Swami X."

"Who?" he shouted again as if he were hard of hearing, although he could not have been more than thirty.

"Swami X," I repeated.

"*Him*. What could you want with *him?* Are you the case-worker?"

"No. I'd just like to talk with him."

"Talk with him? What for?" Suddenly he looked very sad. "I thought you might've come to see me. I do these paintings. No one ever comes to see them. They're of the Holocaust ... Treblinka, Bergen-Belsen ... neorealist portraits of the chambers exactly as they were, taken from original photographs."

"Maybe some other time. Where's the Swami?"

"He doesn't live here anymore."

"Do you know where he moved?"

"No. He disappeared over a year ago. *Adresse unbekannt,* as they say. Address unknown. Return to sender."

"Jesus," I said.

"Why do you say 'Jesus'?" he said. "You're Jewish, aren't you?"

"It's just an expression."

"So the Swami's gone. That's not surprising. He probably killed himself. Every genius kills himself eventually. This is a kingdom of the dumb. You sure you don't want to see my paintings? You know, it's funny. Someone else was here yesterday, looking for him."

"A short black guy, wears a baseball cap turned backward?" Outside, I could see Fouad's cab whistle past.

"Yeah, that was him. He got real upset when he found out the Swami was gone. I thought he was going to have a breakdown or something. He didn't want to see my paintings either. Neither did his friend."

"His friend? Who was his friend?"

"Some creep called Kid Siena. He said I should know who he was because he was a famous graffiti artist. What an ego! I mean, graffiti art isn't art. It's just decoration. A few bright colors on a subway car. You know what I think? All those black and Latino rebels secretly wish they were on Madison Avenue. One call from an ad agency and—"

"Any idea where I could find Kid Siena?"

"How should I know? Defacing the Museum of Modern Art, probably. Now if you'll excuse me, I have *serious* work to do." He turned and disappeared off the landing.

Slowly I opened the wire glass door of the building. Vesey Street was empty. It had started to rain and a small puddle was already reflecting the blurred neon of Shannon's Bar. I waited for Fouad on the stoop. It didn't take long. In about thirty seconds he came skidding around the corner like the front runner at Le Mans. His back door was already open. It was easy to see why: the van was thirty yards behind him and gaining. I dove into the back, slamming hard against the seat and reawakening my fragile ribs just as a shell came crashing through the rear window, splattering tiny pellets of safety glass all over the rear of the cab. I interrupted Fouad, who was muttering imprecations in Arabic at twice the speed of sound.

"The Harvard Club," I shouted.

"What?"

"Forty-fourth Street. I need to make a phone call and it's the safest place I can think of."

The van had disappeared from view by the time we hit the traffic on Eighth Avenue. I did my best to clean up the backseat while reassuring Fouad all repairs would be taken care of. For some peculiar reason he was laughing. "This like old days with Red Cross. Fouad dodge grenade, dodge Uzi, run roadblock. One time go right through gate American Embassy, crash into guardhouse."

We pulled up in front of the Harvard Club with still no visible sign of the van, but I knew he couldn't be far away. Indeed, if he was truly a professional, he would have changed vehicles by now. Whatever he was up to, he would probably restrain himself in this bastion of bourgeois meritocracy. The only paid assassins around here were of the boardroom kind.

I left Fouad double-parked outside and walked straight in with the swagger of an up-and-coming member of the Class of '75. My father had been a graduate, actually, and I had gone there many times as a boy. I knew precisely where the phones were, or used to be, over by the cloakroom. I could see they were occupied for the moment, and I stood at the edge of the lounge, staring across at the portentous portraits of famous alumni: Teddy Roosevelt, FDR, JFK. I used to feel contemptuous of the pomposity of the place and critical of the value system upon which it was based, but this time I felt ill-at-ease, almost overwhelmed by a sense of inferiority as some nameless gumshoe off on a ridiculous wild-goose chase across New York. Almost as quickly, that same sense segued into a feeling of uncontrollable rage. And then I had the first hallucination of my life: among the gallery of portraits, somewhere between a president and a Nobel Prize winner, was my father, in his Wall Street suit, holding an attaché case and staring down at me with a look of extraordinary disapproval. My head swam and my face flushed and I felt like running up and smashing the painting, when my father's image suddenly started to cry. Just as suddenly, I realized where I was, shook myself a few times, walked into a now open phone booth, and called my younger son. I was still trembling as I dialed his number.

"Hello, Simon."

"Hi, Dad. You in New York?"

"Yeah." It was soothing to hear his voice, grounding.

"How is it?"

"Adventurous. How's school?"

"I dunno."

"Not so great, huh? What is it? Math again? Negative numbers? I'll help you when I get back."

"Yeah. I was by your apartment. There was a woman there. She says she's working with you. Not bad, Dad."

"Chantal."

"She's a good cook, too. Made me some chocolate stuff. Profit rolls? She said she used to be a chef."

"Profiteroles. Look, Simon, I need your help on something. Ever hear of a graffiti artist named Kid Siena?"

"Oh, yeah, Dad. He's *fresh*. Kid Siena—wow. He did some bad burners on the Woodlawn Line by the 180th Street station. It all got buffed, though. You know—erased. You met *him?*"

"No. But I'm looking for him. Do you know where he lives?"

"Un-unh. Those guys, you know. They move around a lot."

"Yeah. I know. How about his real name? Do you know that?"

"Kid Siena? . . . I think . . . no."

"What about that book you have, *The Lords of Hip-Hop*? Maybe it's in there?"

"Yeah, yeah. Right. Hold on."

While Simon went for his book, I glanced over at the bulletin board of coming club events. Thursday night they offered a sushi bar, a retrospective of Godard films, and a lecture on debentures. Something for everyone. In a second Simon was back on the line. "Here it is, Dad. I got it. Kid Siena . . . Jorge Mariposa."

"George Butterfly," I said.

"What?"

"That's what it means. Jorge Mariposa is George Butterfly in Spanish. No wonder he changed it to Kid Siena."

"Yeah. That's weak," said Simon. "Anything else you wanna know?"

"That's about it," I said, already thumbing through the
M's in the Bronx directory.

"Guess I gotta do that math now, huh?" He sounded as
if he were headed for forty years in the gulag. I thought of
his brother, who ripped through his homework in about fifteen minutes, and felt bad for him.

"Guess you do."

I said good-bye and hung up just as a group of alums
from what looked like the Class of aught-seven shuffled
through the lobby from the main dining room. They exited
the front door to reveal my friend from the van standing in
an alcove about fifty feet away from me. He didn't say anything, but nodded to me with the apparent warning that, at
least in this city, there was no escaping him, and walked out.

I continued to search the directories, finally finding a
Jorge Mariposa in Manhattan on Columbus Avenue. Judging
by the address, it must have been in the Nineties.

"What it like in there?" said Fouad as we drove uptown
along Central Park West.

"Lot of old farts nodding out, lot of young farts on the
hustle. Pretty dull in all, but it does have a good cigar stand.
Anyway, it's safe."

"Don't take it amiss, but in Beirut that the first kind of
place we blow up."

"We? I thought you were with the Red Cross."

He said something in reply, but I was too busy checking
behind me for the guy in the van, trying to figure which
vehicle he was driving now and who his accomplice was,
because I doubted he was working alone. Or maybe that was
just paranoia. But then I remembered the wry definition of

a paranoid Nathanson had once given me in therapy: someone who knew all the facts. Therapy. I hadn't thought of it
in a couple of days. If what it lead to was having visions of
my father hanging from the wall of the Harvard Club, maybe
it wasn't such a great idea.

The address on Columbus Avenue turned out to be a mid-
dling housing development on Ninety-fifth Street, the kind
of place that brought together junior Columbia faculty and
upwardly mobile Puerto Rican accountants in a common devotion to rent control. Apparently Jorge Mariposa wasn't
doing too badly for a graffiti artist. Maybe he was one of
those I had read about who had gone big-time with museum
sales, gallery representation, and dinner at Elaine's. Or perhaps it was something else.

I found him listed as apartment 9F on the building register, but when I pressed the buzzer next to his name, there
was no answer. I pretended to fumble through the local
throwaway paper until a couple of women who resembled
Aunt Sonya entered with shopping bags. Giving them my
best "I'm-no-mugger" smile while mumbling something
about the unspeakably high price of sturgeon, I drifted in
after them as they unlocked the lobby door. Then I let them
take their own elevator and rode up to the ninth floor alone,
emerging in a grimy, institution-green corridor, my feet
echoing off the worn marble floor. I had come a long way
in my search for Otis King.

I don't think I would have gotten any further had the
Satuloff family been spending that particular Wednesday
evening in a state of domestic tranquillity. But from the
looks of things, the Satuloff family didn't spend too many

evenings in that state. Two minutes after arriving on the ninth floor, I was standing by the incinerator, studying the names on the doors and trying to decide which one to knock on first, when Mrs. Satuloff and then Mr. Satuloff came stomping in and out of their apartment, alternatively slamming the door in the other's face as if this were their nightly ritual. The Satuloff kids were visible across the living room, looking on like spectators at a bullfight. It was ultimately Mrs. Satuloff, a tall woman in a blue reindeer sweater and penny loafers, who came to rest out in the corridor with the door finally, or semifinally, shut behind her.

"One of those nights, huh?" I offered.

"You know the problem with men today," she said. "They want you to be everything—wife, mother, wage earner, support system, priest, rabbi, and mistress."

"It's their revenge for the women's liberation movement."

"You're not kidding," she said. "My first husband was so threatened by my working, I had to pretend I was a housewife when we went to dinner parties. My second husband wants me to earn more money, so I took two jobs and now *he* hates me. I wonder what my third husband will be like."

"An ax murderer?"

"Sometimes I think it'd be better that way. At least I'd know where I stood. You know what the problem is now? We're all living in a sexual netherworld and nobody knows what the hell to do. You ever talk to your average sixteen-year-old kid today? They don't know if they're male, female, or kangaroo."

"I know what you mean. We got a guy right on this hall named Jorge Mariposa."

"Oh, yeah, well, him. That's a different matter. Nothing to do with sex whatsoever. Or not directly."

I didn't know what she meant, so I just nodded.

"I don't think we've met. I'm Alice Satuloff."

"I'm a cousin of the Freemans." I picked a name off the nearest door.

"God, they're ancient. You deserve extra points for coming around and spending time with them."

"I'm just an old-fashioned guy. What about this Mariposa? I saw him a couple of times. What does he do?"

"Well, I can't really say for sure. And I'm not really into local gossip. You know, people who live in glass houses . . ."

"I know what you mean. But every time I'm here, he seems to be coming in the same time I'm going to work. Seven A.M."

She grinned. "That must be closing time at the Club Los Cocos."

"The Club Los Cocos?"

"You must not be from around here."

"I'm not. I'm from, uh, Brooklyn Heights."

She looked at me strangely. "Don't you read *New York* magazine? That new fast-lane place on Ninety-sixth and Columbus where everybody's supposed to—"

Just then the door opened and her husband came out.

"I thought you were dying out here. Who's this?"

"The Freemans' cousin."

"Reilly," I said, pressing the elevator button.

"Reilly? The Freemans have a cousin named Reilly?"

"Yeah. It is funny, isn't it?"

"They never mentioned having a cousin at all."

"He doesn't know about the Club Los Cocos."

"That's weird."

"Why's it weird? Not everybody on the Upper West Side is a coke fiend. Some of us have healthier ways of dealing with our depression, don't we?"

"Are you implying something, Alice?"

"I'm not implying anything. I'm just stating what is obviously the case."

"What is obvious to you is not particularly obvious to me."

"Oh, yeah? Well, why don't you tell that to the guidance counselor at the Ethical Culture School who had to tell you after fourteen years of family life that your *own* daughter . . ."

At that point I got in the elevator.

11

The Club Los Cocos was like a bad set from *Miami Vice,* with mirrored peach glass walls and ten-foot-tall brushed aluminum palm trees that looked like they were borrowed from some department store window. All the men were dressed up in cream-colored suits and white T-shirts like Don Johnson, and the ladies weren't wearing much of anything at all. They were dancing to a frenetic salsa band that was moving up and down at an irregular pace on an elevated platform.

I surveyed the room, trying to choose the right person to guide me to Mariposa, when the sight of someone who was hard to miss made that search irrelevant: Otis himself was dancing by one of the aluminum palm trees. He looked wired to the ceiling as his feet spun around and his arms flailed in every direction doing some whacked-out combination of the pachanga and the kazatsky with two Puerto Rican girls and anyone else who cared to join in. With his celebrity and his zaniness he was making the evening for about half the people in the room as well as for several burly Los Cocos bouncers in orange mesh tank tops who looked on from a ramp by the side of the bandstand.

I made my way over to him, edging my way through the dancers, but he spotted me before I could get him. "Ah, it's Brother Dick! Brother Big Dick! I heard you was lookin' for me. . . . Stop the music, you spic, wop motherfuckers!" he shouted to the band. "We gotta stop this salsa shit for just one second. C'mon stop, José, Carlos, Luis, Miguel, or whatever your name is. Stop!" They stopped. Everyone in the room turned and faced Otis, who was walking toward me, his face dripping with sweat. He put his arm around my shoulder, hanging on me in stoned weariness. "Everybody," he cried out, "this white boy done come all the way from Los Angeles, California, to see me." He looked me straight in the eyes. "Well, you seen me, now *fuck off!*"

"All right. I'll leave." I made a move to go.

"Hey, my man, just kiddin' you. Can't you take a joke?" Otis flashed a sweet, little-boy smile. "What you wanna do, anyway? Carry me back to El Lay, make some people *rich*, play 1980s Stepin' Fetchit for the moo-vee companies? Yes, massa. Yes, massa. Lawdy, lawdy.'' He wiggled his hands like a Holy Roller. "That's who I am, man—Stepin' Fetchit. Ain't no difference 'cept I say motherfucker and talk about how big my dick is. That's what white folks love nowadays, cursin' niggers. How you think Eddie and Richard got so big? You don't see white dudes sayin' shit like that. Not even Sylvester Slambo Stallone. Not even motherfuckin' Belushi said that kind of shit 'less he was imitating black people. You want to laugh at us more, motherfucker? You wanna see me dance? You wanna see me tap? You wanna see me shuck and jive and get so stoned I can't even stand up and my life is a tragedy you write about in one of your books of motherfuckin' sociology I can't even read 'cause I got dyslexia and that ain't all? You want *that?*'' He grabbed my lapels. "Well, then, laugh, motherfuckah, *laugh!*'' he screamed at the top of his lungs and then clutched his stomach, doubling over in pain.

"You all right?''

"Yeah, yeah, man, don't worry about it.'' He tried to smile again, but he kept holding his stomach. "I just got a little bit of an ulcer, I read backward, and I got a heart murmur. Other than that I'm fine. And I gotta go to the bathroom, man.'' Still doubled over, he started heading toward the back of the club. Everybody was staring at him now and I could see the bouncers moving in.

"It's okay,'' I yelled. "I'll take care of him.'' And I pushed him through to the back, into the men's room.

He locked it behind us. "Okay, man, where's the blow?''

"I don't have any.''

"C'mon, don't give me that bullshit. Every white dude in El Lay looks like you does coke. And don't tell me you don't, 'cause then I know you're a liar and I ain't never gonna trust you."

"Yeah, I've done coke. But I wouldn't give you any, Otis."

"C'mon, man, don't be difficult. You gimme a little toot, you tell all your buddies back home you did nose candy with the famous Otis King. That make you one down white boy with a lotta class. The presidents of two fuckin' movie studios was beggin' me to do coke with them. Little Jewish boys just like you. One of them had a picture of Martin Luther King on his office wall."

"I'm here to take you back to Malibu, Otis."

"You wanna take me back to that fascist motherfucker Bannister and you ain't gonna give me some coke? That's no way to build a relationship. You got no sense of social etiquette, my man."

"I thought you liked Bannister."

"Liked Bannister? I was playin' along with the motherfucker. How'd you like to be locked in handcuffs half the day while listening to some bullshit about your mother? Motherfucker treats me like an infant and then expects me to be a grown-up. Hey, man, don't worry about it. C'mon, please please please. Just one little snort. When Kid Siena gets back, he'll pay you back double, triple, give you one of them big, juicy white rocks just for yourself, make you feel like your own Prudential Life Insurance advertisement, know what I mean?"

Just then there was a sudden *bam!* and the bathroom door

flew open. The van driver was standing there, his hand buried deep in his pigskin suede jacket right at the bulge of what I guessed to be a .38.

"Who the fuck is *that?*" said Otis.

"Get outta here, nigger shit." He lifted Otis by the shirt front and pitched him out the door. Then he reached for the .38, but I didn't wait to see it. I ran straight at him, ramming him into the side of the bathroom, the mirror collapsing to the floor. Then I made an attempt to knee him in the groin, but he was too strong for me. He grabbed me by the shoulder and spun me around, hurling me toward the toilet and pulling out his gun in one motion. He raised it to eye level, about to blow me away, when I heard shouting from the club. One of the Los Cocos bodyguards appeared at the bathroom door, and the driver wheeled about instantly and slammed him across the face with the butt of his gun, sending the bodyguard flying back into the club on his knees like a splayed turkey. People started screaming and running for their lives. Before he could turn back to me, I held my breath and dove through the milk glass bathroom window, no idea what was on the other side.

It proved to be a row of garbage cans, some of them unfortunately without their tops. I bounced off them right where my ribs had cracked, then rolled behind a few of the cans just as three shots from an automatic went whistling past me. I didn't know whether to run or pray or piss in my pants. I didn't do any of them but edged farther behind the cans, pressed my body against the ground, and lay as still as I could. The air was misting slightly and the pavement was still damp from the rain. I heard the driver climbing out of the window and then two solid thuds as he landed on the ground what sounded like fifty feet away. I stuck my hand in the open garbage can nearest me but couldn't find anything more helpful than some left-over onion rings.

The driver began surveying the area, walking first down the alley, then back in my direction, the soles of his feet slapping the wet asphalt. I twisted silently onto my back and slid my arm into the next garbage can. It felt damp and putrid, but I was in no mood to be fastidious. I fumbled through what seemed like yesterday's Caesar salad and then something mushy like au gratin potatoes, when my hand hit hard wood. A handle. I didn't know how long it was or what it was, but there was no research time left. The man was within ten feet of me now. I grabbed the handle, rolled to my right, jumped forward and swung, smashing him across the nose. I could hear a sharp crack along his bridge as he cried out and the gun went off, crumbling brick behind me. This was survival time. I kicked him straight in the nuts and slammed him in the jaw again with the handle. He went flying backward, then crumpled against the garbage can, blood flowing rapidly from his nose, his head lolling forward. I slammed him one more for security, dove for his gun, and grabbed it. It was a Walther automatic. I stuffed it under my jacket; then I looked at my own weapon. It was a plumber's plunger. I tossed that away and stooped over the man, patting him down for identification. I found his wallet, but not surprisingly there was nothing in it except about a thousand dollars in cash. I stuck that back in his pocket, then checked his neck and face for any identifying marks. There was nothing remarkable, so I ripped open his shirt. A series of small orderly burn scars ran across his muscular chest from his left pectoral down to his belly button. I was no expert, but it sure looked as if at some point in his life this sonofabitch had been tortured.

He was just starting to come to and took a groggy swipe at me when I heard police sirens. I pushed him back into the garbage cans again and ran around the side of the building into the back of the club through the kitchen. The police were coming in the front and you could feel the anxiety level in the room rising about ten thousand percent. The crowd started making for the bathroom like a swarm of lemmings heading over the hill. Taken together, I figured they could dump enough cocaine to rip the collective lids off the New York sewers. But there was only one toilet in the john, and they were backed up at the door worse than at a Springsteen concert.

I found Otis clutching his arm behind one of the aluminum palm trees. "I need a doctor," he groaned.

"You're also gonna need a lawyer if you don't get your ass out of here as soon as possible." I led him rapidly by his good arm through the kitchen again.

"All right, boys and girls. What is this? Substance Abuse Central? Against the wall!" I heard one of the cops shouting as we ducked out the back door.

Fouad was on the corner of Ninety-fifth and Columbus, where I had left him. Otis was too stoned or hurt to object, so I eased him into the backseat and the Arab shot out of there like the experienced ambulance driver he was. "Saw what you did with van driver," he said as we careened across

110th Street to the Mt. Sinai emergency room. "Good work. Remind me of Christian militia in Shiite refugee camp."

Otis's broken arm proved to be nothing more than a bad bruise and we were on the road to the airport in forty-five minutes. Whatever protests he had about leaving New York had dissolved in the confusion and the Valium they had given him at Mt. Sinai. His usual idling speed of eighty thousand rpm had revved down to a somewhat normal forty.

"Don't take me amiss," Fouad told him as we headed out the Van Wyck Expressway toward Kennedy, "but that movie you make—what they call it?—*Otis Goes Maui*—was for idiot."

"Hey, man. It was for kids."

"Kids not idiots. Fouad know. He have four kids. Kids like computer. Garbage in/garbage out. But you not know about that. I am sure."

Otis leaned into me. "Who the fuck *is* this dude? PLO? I thought you was Jewish."

"Most movies insult children. They think children be stupid, so they make children stupid. People stupid who make the movies. That who stupid."

"Hey, man, I'm tryin' to be a serious artist—a social satirist. Make a statement, know what I mean?"

"Only statement that movie make is where is popcorn. Bad popcorn anyway, filled with additives. Children die of cancer at twenty-five. Don't take me amiss."

"American Airlines," I said.

I left Fouad with five hundred in traveler's checks when he dropped us at the terminal. I also took his phone number.

I wasn't sure exactly why, but some unformed feeling told me it would be useful to have a potential Lebanese ally rattling around New York.

"Don't take it amiss," he said just as Otis and I were about to enter the building, "but you should have killed that driver. In my country they say if man get sentimental about murder, he live to regret it."

12 Otis insisted on flying first class back to L.A. It was in all his contracts, he said. Who was I to disagree? It wasn't my money. So we sat there in the wide leather seats eating mediocre chateaubriand and drinking Courvoisier from a full liter bottle a fawning stewardess had placed in front of him as we jetted through the night sky. With everything he had put in his body in the last twenty-four hours, by the time the pilot announced we were flying over Cleveland, the cognac had him speaking in tongues. I'd ask him a question and get back an answer in what Jack Kerouac, desperate to be identified with jazz musicians, used to call "spontaneous boprosity." I told him, but he had never heard the term.

"You know what it is with you liberal white boys," he said, finally coming down to planet Earth or wherever we were after a sugar rush from the chocolate sundae. "You worship black people so much, it make us crazy. Y'all think you be black, everything be great. No problems. No responsibilities. Get laid every other minute. But if you was black, you'd hate it."

"Was Mike like that?"

"Worse case I ever saw. Talkin' jive all the time. Listenin' to worn-out Motown shit and eatin' ribs till it made you sick. Never saw the motherfucker shake hands straight in his life. He always be high-fivin' you to death like he was Magic Johnson. And lately it was Africa, Africa, Africa, everywhere he went. I told him he liked Africa so much he should go live in Nigeria for a while, see how much he like it."

"Did he ever go?"

"Yeah, he went. For about a week. With his old lady. On a mission for that Africa aid la-dee-dah guilt trip she be runnin' down. Bought himself a safari suit and one of them wide-brim hats with the zebra band from Abercrombie and Fitch and got his ass videotaped next to a scrawny water buffalo and some half-dead Ethiopian kids with the fat bellies."

"Why don't you like her?"

"Who?"

"Emily."

"Because she all bullshit, man. She just doin' it to make herself feel good. She don't give a flying fuck about no black kids. All she wants is her name on the charity letter. In big print, right at the top."

"Is that so bad if she gets them the money?"

"I don't know. Fuck." He emptied the cognac bottle into his glass and downed it. Then his expression turned plaintive, almost lost, as if there were no bottom to his sadness.

"Did Mike ever mention anything to you about some twenty-five million dollars?"

"Who told you that?" Otis suddenly sat up straight. "My brother? You ain't gonna do nothin' to my brother, are you, man? He's all I got in the world, 'cause Della won't see me. I love her so much, I'd marry her for life and write it in stone on my heart, but she won't talk to me unless I kick for six months. She wants me to get a fuckin' doctor's certificate. Now how'm I gonna get that?"

"Maybe Bannister."

"Yeah, Bannister. All's I gotta give 'im for that is my balls, my career, and my freedom. . . . Well, that ain't so bad." He grinned at me. "At least I'll have my woman!"

"What about the money?"

"What money?"

"The twenty-five million."

"Oh, that bullshit story. I told you how bad Mike wanted to be hip. It was all part of that, tryin' to be a black, underworld motherfucker and makin' up some fairy tale about blood money and Mafia shit."

"Is that what it was? Mafia shit?"

"I don't know. I just made *that* up. All's I know is Mike made it up too, tryin' to be important. He never said a word to me until he knew our partnership was dead. It was like he was braggin' or something. You know—if I was gonna get rich, he was gonna get rich too. But he was all fucked up. He didn't know what's obvious to anybody. Money don't count for shit after ya got enough to eat, 'cause it won't buy ya love. And if yo mama didn't love ya, ya ain't ever gonna get it anyway, so screw you. It's all a black comedy—and I do mean *black.*" He laughed. "I didn't need no Bannister to tell me that. I found out the truth fo' myself when I was three years old and my mama leave me alone in the apartment to turn tricks and come back three days later, me pissin' on the floor and eatin' Wonder Bread and Kool-Aid out of the refrigerator till the can run out. And that bitch Della don't want me now either. But she says it's *my fault.* It ain't my fault. It's a conspiracy. You know what? Sometimes I think we live in a conspiracy of bitches.''

Otis wanted to join the conspiracy the moment we got off the plane and he saw Chantal waiting for us by the gate.

"This your woman?"

"Assistant, er, uh, partner."

"Thank *God* for *that.* " He stared at Chantal with a smile of almost embarrassingly open rapture. " 'Cause I'm in love, baby. Cupid just hit me with one of them incredible darts. Wait a minute. Wait a goddamned minute. Didn't I see you onstage at the Fun Zone a coupla weeks ago? You're a comic *genius!* Oh, help me, help me, Jesus, Satan, somebody, I been stung. I ain't ever gonna get out of this motherfucker." He made a charming little-boy face at Chantal, who blushed in spite of herself.

"How do you do?" she said.

"I dunno. You tell me. How'm I doin'?"

"Working a little too hard," I said.

"Hey, this motherfucker jealous. And he don't even have a reason. C'mon, baby. Let's give him a reason." He took Chantal by the arm and started off toward the exit with her. "How's your career goin', baby? You know, I know the dude at *The Merv Griffin Show.* He might be interested in your act. 'Bout time they had a few more women on there. Support the ERA, y'know what I mean?"

Otis kept going right to the car. I couldn't believe Chantal would fall for a rap like that, but I couldn't shrug it off. Otis was right. I was jealous. In fact, as we drove out of the lot, I felt about ready to throttle him.

"Y'know what, baby?" He leaned over the front seat and put his hand on her shoulder. "I been thinkin'. Next spring I got this World War Two flick in Italy with Giancarlo Giannini and—"

"Thanks, Otis, but no thanks." She took his hand off her shoulder and placed it on the seat. "I quit show business and I'm staying quit. Being a private investigator is more interesting. It's about real life."

I looked over at her and smiled, but she just shrugged.

"Oh, I get it," said Otis. "You guys got eyes for each other, but you don't have the balls to admit it. That just like white people."

And with that he went to sleep in the backseat.

Chantal and I didn't say a word to each other until we were almost in Malibu.

"Is he out?" she asked, glancing back at Otis as we passed the Getty Museum.

"He ought to be."

"Okay." She looked back at him again just to make sure, then took out a note pad. "Your friend on the Asian Squad says the Chu's Brothers are scavengers. They used to hang around the Rampart Division trying to get information from the cops."

"Police blotter groupies."

"What they were after here, I haven't been able to find out. Ditto for Stanley Burckhardt at the Glendale post office, but he's still trying. As for Bannister, things seem to have been pretty normal at his compound, but I wasn't watching it that much of the time because—here's the interesting thing—I think Emily Ptak is having an affair."

"Really? Who with?"

"I'm not sure. All I know is I followed her from her house this afternoon straight to the Bonaventure Hotel in downtown L.A. She didn't know me, so I rode up to the seventh floor with her on that glass elevator they have. She walked to Room Seven-fifteen, knocked, and said 'It's me.' Someone opened the door a crack and she slipped inside."

"Did you try to get in?"

"Of course I did." She looked annoyed I had even asked. "Ten minutes later I knocked on the door and said it was Housekeeping, but Emily yelled back they didn't want anything. An hour later I dialed them on the house phone and said it was the switchboard and we were having a computer problem. 'Is this Mr. Morgan's room?' The guy said no. I asked, 'Well, then, whose room is it?' and he hung up. I also tried the bell captain, pretending I had a package to deliver, but he wouldn't tell me anything. I guess I could've done better, huh?"

"Not bad," I said. "Fancy hotels are really hard to crack."

"Are you sure? I think I screwed up. I should've figured out something, talked to the chambermaid or the maintenance guy. I mean, my mother was an actress and I grew up in hotels."

"You did fine. You found out more than I knew, and at least we know she's having an affair with a man."

Then jet lag hit and I felt about ten feet underwater by the time I turned into the Malibu Colony. I did manage to find Bannister's place, however. It was almost two in the morning by then, but the psychiatrist was waiting up like an angry parent when we arrived. He sent the Samoan out to the car; he picked up Otis with one arm and carried him toward the door like a Cabbage Patch doll. He set him down on the front step, opposite Bannister.

"I never want you to leave again, Otis."

"I won't, massa. You know that."

"Next time I'll have to take those measures I described to you."

"Uh-huh."

"I'll see you tomorrow morning at six for our usual jog. Be ready."

"What the fuck?" said Otis, who could barely stand up.

"Just because you ran off like a foolish child doesn't mean you'll be allowed to abandon your schedule for one second," said Bannister, who thanked me and followed the Samoan and Otis into the house.

I was having trouble keeping my eyes open, so Chantal drove us back to West Hollywood while I told her what had happened in New York. It should have been a strange experience; it had been a long time since I had shared what I did with anybody other than my shrink. I often thought that I became a private eye because I liked *my* privacy, needed it even, as if the more I exposed of myself, the more I lost. But there I was, telling her everything, every detail from Fouad's driving habits to my outright terror hiding behind the garbage cans in the alley of the Club Los Cocos, and it felt perfectly natural.

"You're lucky you're alive," she said as we turned up Miller Drive and pulled up in front of the apartment.

"Yeah. I suppose. But you don't think about it at the time. You just act."

"Well, I'm really glad you're okay." She looked at me and smiled. "Glad it wasn't any worse."

We didn't say anything for a moment. I could hear the dusky sexuality of a Wynton Marsalis record drifting up from the Strip.

"Come in?" I asked.

"Moses, it's almost three. Besides, you need some rest."

"That's for me to decide."

"Look, Moses, I'd like to, but . . . it's not smart. The last time I slept with my boss was when I was a photographer's assistant in Boston and I got in a horrible situation with his wife and ended up losing my job."

"I haven't been married for ten years."

"That's not the point. It's just not professional. How'm I going to look at you in the morning when we have to go off and investigate something?"

"I don't know. How *are* you going to look at me?"

"What're you going to say if you want me to do something and I disagree and we get into an argument?"

"I hadn't thought about that."

"Well, you'd better think about it."

"Why?"

"Because it's really a problem. This stuff doesn't mix. I've been there. I know."

It was just as well. Twenty minutes later I was fast asleep, a video cassette of *The Best of Mike Ptak* blaring brightly from the television set at the end of my bed.

When you begin to suspect your shrink of being involved in a crime, is this genuine suspicion or resistance to therapy?

I was speculating on that problem as I sat opposite Nathanson the next afternoon. I had just finished telling him about Chantal, about how this French-Canadian woman had walked into my life and how I was feeling euphoric and apprehensive at once, when I noticed a book of matches from the Top of the Five Restaurant at the Bonaventure Hotel on his desk.

"How's the food?" I asked, nodding toward the matches, which were sitting on a volume of licensing requirements from the Board of Medical Examiners.

"What do you mean?"

"The Top of the Five at the Bonaventure. It wasn't bad when I tried it last February. When were *you* there?"

"Is this part of your therapy, Moses?"

"I'm just curious, really. It's always surprising when hotel food is better than—"

"Don't you wonder why, in the middle of discussing what you describe as the most powerful feelings you've had for a woman in some time, you deflect the conversation to neutral territory?"

"Nothing is neutral. Everything has a purpose. Didn't you say that once?"

"Yes. And do you think your purpose here might be to avoid dealing with your emotions?"

"I doubt it. My purpose right now is to get some facts."

"What facts?"

"You weren't, by any chance, on the seventh floor of the Bonaventure Hotel yesterday afternoon?"

Nathanson studied me a moment. "Why do you want to know that?"

"Because Emily Ptak was visiting someone in Room Seven-fifteen."

"I see. . . . And how do you feel about that?"

"How do I *feel* about that? Suspicious as all hell. That's how I feel about that. Her husband's barely two weeks in the ground and she's having clandestine meetings with a man in a suite at the Bonaventure Hotel!"

"And I'm supposed to be that man?"

"It's my job to check out all possibilities."

"Could it be that Emily Ptak left some matches from the Bonaventure Hotel in my office? Her appointment is two hours before yours."

"Yes, it's possible. I just want to know."

"Could it also be possible that Emily Ptak's visit to the Bonaventure had nothing whatever to do with what you think it did?"

"I don't *know* why she went there. But when a woman visits a man in a hotel room in the middle of the day and neither of them acknowledges their presence, it's been my professional experience that they weren't there studying for their Latin test."

Nathanson straightened himself in his chair and regarded

me calmly. "Moses, remember when we discussed 'figure' and 'ground' ... how your own tensions—melancholia, if you will—sometimes prevented you from seeing what was right in front of your eyes?"

"Are you trying to tell me something?"

"Nothing more than I'm saying. Life can be simpler than you make it."

"I'd like to know how."

"Well, for example, what do you want from me? Right here. Now."

"An answer. No more shrink bullshit!"

"And if I gave you one, would you believe it?"

"I'd want to."

"But would you?"

I didn't have an answer.

I left there ten minutes later with my head spinning. The thought of Emily Ptak up there in that hotel room with Nathanson was disconcerting for several reasons, not the least of which was that he was my shrink. Also, he was a cripple. Add the fact that Emily was lying to me. And that Emily was my client and by far the most lucrative one I had had in some time. I was loath to lose her and I didn't like myself for that. The whole thing was making me sick to my stomach and that was too bad because I was headed directly for the Rodman mansion in Bel Air for the Comedians and Chefs Benefit for Africa, and according to that morning's *Los Angeles Times,* the famous Sandor Romulus had been cooking for three days in honor of the occasion.

It was like a German car convention as I handed my keys to the valet and joined the men in overpriced neopunk sport

shirts and the women in unisex silk pajamas at the corner
of Copa de Oro and Braxton. From there we were transferred
into mini-vans and ferried up the private eucalyptus-lined
road that led up to Matthew Rodman's. Even in the van I
got the sense of the crowd as middle-aged, upscale entertainment industry liberals who might once have been at the
barricades, but were a long way from it now, even beyond
the easy nostalgia about Columbia and People's Park I used
to hear at similar events. Now I heard a lot of talk about
deal-making, but it didn't sound much like an old Woody
Allen movie. It was more earnest and deadly, as if there were
only a certain amount of money left on a precarious globe
and only a short time left to get it.

Rodman, a homosexual who had made his fortune in shopping centers, lived in a cool modern castle of seemingly end-
less baronial rooms with white Carrara marble floors and
tiny seashells inlaid in the rough-hewn concrete walls. All
this austerity was counteracted only by a large collection of
Indian miniatures and, today, by hundreds of salami-shaped
salmon and gray helium balloons that were dangling from
the ceiling with the words "Cosmic Aid" printed on them
in elegant black Deco. Two streets signs of the same colors
stood in the living room pointing TO THE COMEDIANS and
TO THE CHEFS. I stood between them, wondering which way
to go, when Emily, in a sixtiesish paisley damask and Chinese
rubber flats, came up and clasped my hand firmly between
hers.

"I don't know how to thank you for what you've done for
us. It would have been such an embarrassment without Otis,
and whatever differences we may have had, I know you've

done him a service too. He's such a talented man and he shouldn't be doomed by his own self-destructiveness. And next you're going to find out why Mike died. Have you had something to eat? Sandor made the most astonishing soufflé of chanterelles on radicchio."

"Maybe later. I'm feeling a little queasy."

"Then you must come and meet Eddy. You know, Eddy Sandollar—the guy behind all this. They call him the Rock 'n' Roll Saint." She took me by the arm and led me across the room to where a slightly overweight man in his early thirties was holding forth to a group of admirers. He wore his long blond hair almost shoulder length in late Beatles style, classic Wayfarer Ray-Bans, and an original Hawaiian shirt that would've made Randy Newman jealous.

"So I told them," he was saying, "don't give me your bureaucratic bullshit. We're talking human survival here. We've got an earthquake in Mexico. Little children are buried alive. Now either give me those medicines or get off the phone and stop wasting my time."

"Excuse me a moment, Eddy," said Emily. "I'd just like you to meet someone—Moses Wine."

"Hey, brother," he turned to me, grabbing my hand in a soul shake. "You're the Fearless Fosdick who brought Otis back to us!" He pulled me in closer to him and whispered, "I know it sounds corny, man, but you saved a soul. Back in the old days we all wanted to 'save the world'—remember the song? But if you help just one man as long as you live, you've saved yourself. That's why I quit the record business. I was getting into such a heavy ego trip I had to get out before it got me."

"Eddy organized the Heavy Metal Hunger Concerto at the Hollywood Bowl last year," said Emily. "They made a fortune."

"I know. I saw the MTV," I said. "That was some all-star lineup you put together, everything from doo-wop to bebop."

"Hey, that wasn't me. I was only the conduit. It only passed through me, as Satchidananda used to say. Besides, it's easy. You put the word out and the managers are climbing all over each other just to get the exposure. So, a private eye, huh?" He studied me for an instant with a kind of weird intensity that was visible even through the Ray-Bans. Then his gaze shifted away almost as quickly. "You've got to meet my wife," he said, taking the hand of a surprisingly plain Oriental woman of about twenty-five in an airbrushed Cosmic Aid T-shirt. "This is Kim. She rescued me when I was stone broke. You know the trip, driving a Rolls and filing Chapter Eleven. Kim transformed me spiritually. Like most of us, I was born in the Judaeo-Christian tradition, but I had to branch out. Then I could stop negating."

Kim didn't say anything.

"Negating what?" I asked.

"The whole thing. The spurious glamour of the music scene—sex, drugs, and rock 'n' roll. I was hooked on ambition. Now I'm hooked on giving. And you know what? It works."

"It does, Moses," said Emily. "It's saved me since Mike died."

"It doesn't make you walk on water, but it helps you sleep nights," said Sandollar. "Hey, have you tried the eats? Sandor Romulus is the next thing in California cuisine, man.

And everything's low-cal—we made sure of that. No choles-
terol, lipids, or any of those carcinogens except the air we
breathe.'' He tossed his head back to get the blond hair out
of his eyes. ''Look, man, I'd love to rap with you all day, a
private dick doing your kind of charity work turns me on,
but I gotta shake the pockets of these characters over here.''
He gestured toward a couple of older gays in crew-neck
sweaters. ''They run the Au Pair Gallery and we're planning
a round of benefits with the art world. Rauschenberg and
Johns have already promised posters. Check you later.''

He grasped my hand and shook it firmly before moving
on to the gallery owners. For the first time I was starting to
feel hungry, as if my duty to the world's starving were to go
tank up on the latest cuisine. I followed the TO THE CHEFS
sign to a buffet table laden with everything from mesquite-
grilled Santa Barbara shrimp to pizza topped with cabernet
grapes and goat cheese. And despite what Sandollar had
said, there were also enough brioches, croissants, and bagels
to distend the stomach of any California bulimic whose binge
cycle ran to outré restaurants and whose purge cycle ran to
self-flagellating exercise classes.

I was filling my plate and watching Sandor Romulus, a
short, trim man in white pants and a black T-shirt, hold
court behind the table like Le Roi Soleil himself while a
couple of forlorn movie stars languished nearby in uncomfortable anonymity when Chantal came up beside me. She
looked terrific in a silver camisole with a cameo just above
her right breast.

''My shrink says I can't distinguish between 'figure' and
'ground,' '' I told her. ''Which one are you?''

"Both." She smiled.

"Well, I can see the figure, but how about the ground?"

"All things come to those who wait—even a smartass." She slipped her arm in mine. "Come on. You're missing Otis."

"Have you seen Bannister?" I asked as she led me out the building in the direction of a temporary stage that had been erected on the tennis court in front of a large video screen.

"Not yet."

"Funny. I didn't think he'd be late for an event like this. It's loaded with potential clients."

We arrived at the back of the crowd and edged our way toward the stage. Otis was standing there with a microphone in his hand looking straight out of *Interview* magazine in a dinner jacket and jeans with a tieless tuxedo shirt. "I had to clean up my act," he was saying to the appreciative audience. "We're talkin' about poverty here, and just because there are fifty studio executives at this party who can *fire* my ass don't mean I'm not here for *one* reason only—to feed the bellies of starvin' babies. So no motherfucker or pussy jokes." There was a round of nervous laughter that died off quickly, perhaps too quickly, and Otis realized it. "But seriously, folks," he continued, "dirty words are not the killers in this world. Dirty acts are. And one of the dirtiest acts around is not feedin' people when there's plenty to go around. And I'm not just talkin' about that orange juice pizza you people been eatin' out there. Don't you think that's weird? The more people die in Africa, the stranger the food is we eat. Pretty soon the whole continent'll be dead

over there and you'll be eating ice cream with Worcester-
shire sauce." Laughter. "Now isn't that just my style? In-
sultin' the hell out of the white people and makin' 'em laugh.
You be a bunch of masochists, huh? And what that make
me—the Marquis de Spade? So open up your wallets, ma-
sochist babies, and call your accountants, 'cause the man
I'm about to introduce to you deserves all your attention
and all your money. And I do mean *all!* I'm talkin' about
none other than the man that rocked and rolled, funky-
chickened, jerked, and slam-danced right into your pockets—the Michael Jackson, Bruce Springsteen, Prince, and
Mick Jagger of international aid ... Fast Eddy Sandollar."

"Thanks, Otis," said Sandollar, taking the microphone
from the comedian, who remained on the stage with him. "I
think we'd all rather be insulted by you than praised by a
lot of the moral hypocrites who are around these days. Now
I know most people out here have gone through a lot—we
had a dream with Martin, we had a New Frontier with Jack,
and a Great Society with Lyndon. And although some of
those dreams faded, I've gotta tell you—look around—we
don't have it so bad. But I also don't have to tell you that
there are a lot of people out there who don't have it so good.
Putting it bluntly, there's a second Holocaust going on, and
the scene of that Holocaust isn't Buchenwald, Auschwitz, or
Bergen-Belsen; it's Ethiopia, the Sudan, and Mali. You say
Holocaust is a big word? Well, let me tell you, I didn't realize how bad it was myself a few years back when I was
sitting in my penthouse office as president of Licorice Records, listening to demos and smoking dope. So at the risk of

boring people who spend their days watching dailies and rough cuts—''

"Bore 'em, Eddy," shouted Otis. "Bore the shit out of 'em. Then we'll give 'em some more of that strawberry pizza with garlic cookies and they'll be all set to go again."

"Sounds good, Otis." Sandollar nodded to an aide, who switched on the video projector. An image of a barren desert appeared on the screen. "This is East Africa. According to the United Nations Economic and Social Council, twelve million people there are on the verge of extinction. It is the greatest human need crisis of our time." The camera turned 180 degrees to reveal about a dozen near naked, sad-eyed waifs who looked as if they were all suffering from infectious diseases or acute malnutrition. "To avert this catastrophe, if it's not already too late, we need to triple our contributions of medical supplies and food." Several of the children, flies buzzing around their heads, stretched their hands out to the camera, imploring the audience directly for aid. It was hard to watch. "We need to do it now. And we need to avoid the greedy, corrupt local politicians, whether they be Marxist, capitalist, fascist, or whatever." As Sandollar continued, I had the odd sensation people were pushing their way through the crowd, causing it to shift about. "So we have come to you, the members of the community that is historically the most generous because your creative gifts make you the most closely attuned to the suffering of others." The shifting continued and I turned to my left, noticing Koontz edging his way toward the stage. Behind him were Estrada and another plainclothes detective in a black leather jacket and Carrera glasses. "And it is that suffering I call upon you to alleviate, to commit yourselves to alleviating not just once, but on a continuing basis." I turned to see three more policemen in uniform stationed in the back. "We don't want to be cultural or even intellectual imperialists. We just want to give them the money and materials directly so they can help themselves." I turned forward again. Koontz had reached the stage and was talking with Otis, who was staring down at him with a puzzled expression. "In these days we have to fight cynicism; we have to fight inertia. There is hope. We *can* make a better world. In the words of John Lennon: 'Imagine!' "

Koontz said something else and Otis tensed, moving to his right a couple of steps. Suddenly he bolted from the stage, running across the tennis court like a halfback digging for the goal line. As he did so, the three uniformed cops started sprinting to the fence gate ahead of him. Otis jumped backward and spun around only to find Koontz and his cronies right behind him.

"What the hell kind of bullshit is this?" Otis's voice suddenly boomed out over the crowd like a small dynamite explosion. "These cops is crazy! Get the hell out of here!"

"I'm sorry, folks. Sorry to inconvenience you here," said Koontz as he and Estrada each took Otis firmly by an arm. "We wanted to do this more quietly."

"Fuck quiet! This is bullshit! This is racism! You been tryin' to kill me since I was born!"

Otis took a wild swing at the third detective, who reached for a pair of cuffs and started to clap them on him as Koontz and Estrada grabbed his arms and pulled them back again.

"I'm sure you know your rights under the *Miranda* decision, Mr. King."

I pushed my way forward through the astonished crowd.

"Jesus Christ, Koontz, what're you doing? We're not in Needle Park here."

"I'm doing what I have to, Wine. What the taxpayers pay me to do." He stared at me sharply. I looked around at the crowd. Everybody looked as stunned as I was.

"C'mon, Koontz." I tried to lower my voice. "You can't take a man like this away in front of all these people. You're going to ruin his career. Give him a break. Besides, he's under twenty-four-hour psychiatric care. He's not going anywhere."

"Twenty-four-hour psychiatric care, huh?"

"Yes. With Dr. Carl Bannister. In Malibu."

"Well, Wine, from here on in I don't think anybody's gonna be under Bannister's care, whatever it was worth. Because he was found dead about four hours ago. And as of this moment, Otis King is under arrest for his murder."

14 "How long do you figure he was in the bushes?" asked Jacob, my older son. We were sitting around my kitchen table—he, Chantal, Simon, Aunt Sonya, and I—eating a plain, ordinary pepperoni pizza five hours after the Comedians and Chefs Benefit for Africa broke up with large quantities of untouched gourmet food, including mine, sitting on the flower-strewn picnic tables.

"Supposedly they went jogging at six A.M. That's the schedule, anyway. They run out the gates of the Colony, across the PCH, and up into the hills in an area called the Serra Retreat."

"I know that place," said Simon, who often went surfing in Malibu Lagoon. "There are some ranches up there. Lots of eucalyptus trees."

"And so they say the black man killed the white man with a knife," said Sonya. "This is not so very different from the Scottsboro Boys."

"Oh, come on," I said. "That was 1931. They couldn't get lawyers until the day of the trial and eight of them got death sentences."

"Yes, but they were freed on appeal three years later," said Jacob.

"Wise guy," I said. For the last couple of years Jacob

had often affected a world-weary attitude, as if all of society were dictated by jaded journalists and blasé fashion designers. He and his friends were after security and money. It was their way of rebelling against sixties parents who had themselves lost most of *their* ideals. But, I figured, like everything else, this too would pass. "Anyway," I continued, "this is totally different. A black millionaire is accused of slitting the throat of a white celebrity psychiatrist."

"*That* is a revolutionary act," said Sonya.

"Very funny."

"So what *is* revolutionary? Charity benefits?" Sonya snorted. "They accomplish nothing. Worse—they push things backward. I hate to quote the Bible, but it was all in the Fifth Book of Ecclesiastes: 'When goods increase, they are increased that eat them.' All charity does is create more people with more starvation and more disease. In order to change, a nation must change itself. Now, in China—"

"Okay, okay. I know you just took my son to see a rerun of *The Battle of Algiers,* but this event is about as revolutionary as a stock merger and Otis King is going to have about as thorough a legal defense as John DeLorean."

"So you think he's guilty." This was Chantal.

"I didn't say that. But either the police are stupider than I think they are or whoever set Otis up is a bloody genius, because nobody would have pulled in a man like that on such short notice without a helluva case. And look at what we already know they have: a murder weapon with Otis's prints on it; yards of motivation from Bannister's case notes stating the details of his brother's criminality and, Koontz intimated to me, Otis's personal involvement in it; several witnesses who saw them running into the woods together and Otis running out by himself; *and* Otis's own extreme paranoid personality and background of child abuse, crime, and drugs.''

"Inadmissible," said Jacob.

"Yes, inadmissible, but not to us if we're trying to figure out if he really did it.''

"What has happened to you?" said Sonya. "Have you turned into one of them?''

"Sonya, this is a millionaire. Not some poor junkie. And if it were some poor junkie who had killed this guy, I'd call it like it is, too. But, all right, I don't think he did it.''

"Ay . . ." Sonya sighed deeply. "You almost gave me a heart attack.''

"But I'm not sure. Let me tell you that.''

"I don't care. At least you haven't turned into one of them. I was scared that therapy had destroyed you.''

"Therapy? Therapy doesn't destroy anybody!" I was so defensive I was almost shouting. Despite the high drama of the past few hours, I was still unable to shake my last session with Nathanson. Even a casual mention of the subject set me off. Chantal looked at me.

"Why don't we calm down and examine some of the facts here?" she said.

"Okay. What about you?" I turned to Simon, who was scribbling some graffiti on the back of my *New Republic*. "Any homework?''

"Some math. An English composition.''

"Go.''

"What?''

"Do it. Just go do it. I don't want to hear about it. And stop using the covers of my magazines for artistic expression. You've got a sketch pad."

I pointed to the bedroom. He glowered at me as he trudged off.

"All right, let's go back to square one."

The phone rang. I picked up. It was Emily.

"Uh, Moses," she said. "I know it's late, but I didn't want you to go off tomorrow morning and waste your day without my talking to you."

"Waste my day?"

"Yes. I don't think I'll be needing your services anymore. As far as I'm concerned, this is all a police matter from here on in and they seem to be doing a satisfactory job. Thank you very much for what you've done. You've been more than adequate professionally, and if you'll send me a bill, I'll of course reimburse you for all your time and expenses, but I don't want you to go any further." She said it all quickly, as if she had rehearsed it.

"Are you sure about this?"

"Absolutely. Good night, Moses. Thank you." She hung up.

"We're fired," I said.

Chantal put her hand to her head. "Wow, this is worse than stand-up comedy. At least there they give you notice. Well, it's been interesting, but brief." She stood and picked up her shoulder bag. "I'll drop the car off in the morning. I'll let you know the gas and mileage. You can send me my check."

"Hey, I didn't say *you're* fired. I said *we're* fired."

"The case is over. What're you going to pay me with, worry beads?"

"Well, you've already put this grandiose message on the machine about International Investigative Consultants. Maybe we should try to live up to it. This is the era of yuppie entrepreneurship, isn't it? For the next six weeks, anyway. It's either that or open a restaurant."

Sonya and Jacob looked at each other. Chantal glanced at them, then slowly sat back down, studying me with an expression halfway between relief and wariness.

"A restaurant sounds like a better idea," said Jacob.

"Thanks for your support," I said.

"You don't have to do me any favors," said Chantal. "I mean, you don't owe me anything."

"I know."

We sat silently for a moment.

"Well," said Sonya finally. "You're going to start your own CIA. How're you going to do that? Go to the bank and get a loan?"

"First we're going to finish the Otis King case. Or the Ptak and King case or whatever it is. It's sure to be big news in L.A., in fact *everywhere,* for the next few months, and whoever breaks it open will get a lot of great publicity."

"Suppose it's already solved?" said Jacob.

"That's a risk we have to take." I lit up a joint and passed it over to Chantal. "Meanwhile, I'll show you how to drum up some business on your own. If it works, if you bring in enough on your own, we'll stick with it. If not . . ."

She nodded, sucking on the joint and passing it over to Sonya, who held it at arm's length. "You still insist on giving me this stuff," she said. "You know I consider it a sign of bourgeois decadence and also this young man is a minor. You're corrupting him."

"I'm seventeen," said Jacob. "At the age of twenty Alexander had already attacked the Persian Empire with thirty-five thousand troops."

"Yeah, and at twenty-three Dennis Kucinich was elected mayor of Cleveland. We all know this is a world of prodigies, but in deference to this woman's age, and to the indisputable fact that we will all be Gray Panthers one day, let's cool it." I took the joint and snuffed it out. "Also, it's almost midnight. Why don't you give your great-aunt a ride home?"

I kissed Sonya good night and gave Jacob a quick hug, and they shook hands with Chantal and left. Then I went into the second bedroom to check on Simon. He was already fast asleep with his head on the unopened math book. I slid it out, took off his shoes, and tucked him in. Then I walked back into the kitchen and sat down opposite Chantal.

"Well, here we are," I said.

"Yes." She looked at me for a moment, then picked up the joint and stared at it. "Your therapist—what did he mean about 'figure' and 'ground'?"

"It's kind of like that old perceptual trick, being able to pick out a pattern in a field of dots. Or the cliché about not seeing the forest for the trees."

"And you don't do that?"

"Sometimes I let my problems interfere. At least he thinks so."

"But that's true for everybody, isn't it?" She turned the joint in her hand and put it down. "My ex would use all those terms—neuro-this, retro-that—for things that were common knowledge anyway. In the end I saw he was using them as a way to control me. At least most of the time." She looked up at me and smiled. "But you do all right the way you are. I can tell."

"Thanks. You do too."

She shrugged, a funny little line curving up just beneath her lower lip and disappearing in the hollow of her cheek.

"You know, it's a long time since I thought I was falling in love with somebody." The words weren't premeditated. They just came out of me from some mysterious place. Like the ground coming out from under the figure—or was it the reverse?

Chantal blushed slightly and looked away. I felt embarrassed too. I didn't say anything until she turned back to me.

"Sorry about that. I didn't mean to ..."

"No. That's okay. Those are just big words and ..."

"You've heard them before."

She nodded. We sat there in the kind of uncomfortable silence they say you can drive trucks through. I could hear her breathing and feel my pulse rate going up. After a while we were staring at each other like a couple of seventeen-year-olds at a drive-in.

"You know, for somebody who was a stand-up comic, you're very shy."

"That's not so strange, is it?"

"No, I guess it's not." I looked at her again. "You wanna break your rule?" I asked.

"Yes."

I took her hand and we walked slowly into my bedroom. In the green light of the neon wall clock, we began to undress each other.

"You're trembling," she said.

"So are you."

"It's not so serious."

"No, it's not. At least I don't think it is."

Our clothes fell to the floor and I could see her body outlined in the closet mirror. It was long and smooth with a soft round butt that curved neatly into white-white thighs. Her pubic hair was the same auburn as her head but coiled in tight little springlike curls against her skin. I wrapped my arms around her and we lowered ourselves onto the bed. And then we made love. The earth didn't move or anything. But considering we had never done it before, and considering what had gone on that day, and considering the battle scars of the participants and that I still couldn't move off my right side because of my mending ribs, considering all that, you could say it was pretty terrific.

The phone rang the next morning at 5:46. It felt like a terrorist attack. I fumbled for it in the dark, almost knocking the radio and lamp off my headboard.

"Hello," I groaned.

"Hello, Mr. Wine."

"Yeah?"

"My name is Nick Steinway—no relation. Would you mind coming down to my office? I'd like to speak with you."

"Speak with me? Do you have any idea what—"

"It's a short day, Mr. Wine. And there's only so much

time to get things accomplished. If you could be over here in, say, fifteen minutes, I'll have you done and out by six-thirty.''

"What is this—a haircut?"

"Cute. Look, Wine, be here. You'll be glad you did."

"Where's here?"

"Global Pictures, Executive Building, Suite Two Hundred. How do you take your eggs?"

"Sunny side."

He hung up.

I looked over at Chantal, who was staring groggily at me. "Go to sleep," I said. "I'll be back in a few minutes." I got up and gave myself the two-minute shave.

At precisely 6:05 that morning I walked through the door that said PRESIDENT, WORLDWIDE PRODUCTION into Nick Steinway's reception room. The way things were operating, it could have been three in the afternoon. Two bearded guys of about thirty were talking anxiously on a white leather couch with an attractive silver-haired woman about ten years their senior while, through an open doorway, a group of four men in suits were visible going over some papers amidst pots of coffee in a dining alcove. But they all seemed to have something in common: they were all rubbing their eyes.

"You must be Mr. Wine," said the secretary, a motherly type in a gray smock. "Mr. Steinway wants to see *you* straight away." She buzzed the inner office. "It's Mr. Wine."

I turned as the office door swung open by itself, or rather by a remote control operated by a short, wiry man in his late twenties seated on another white leather couch, this one about twice the size of the one in the reception room. He was talking on the phone while glancing at about a half-dozen scripts that were stacked on his lap. "He can call me what he wants," I heard him say as he gestured for me to come in. "He's three days behind and he's going to have to cut ten pages." He hung up and stood, shaking my hand. "Mr. Wine, I presume. . . . Just a second. I'll be right with you. . . . Did you get those eggs?" But before I could answer he walked right past me into the reception room. "Have you solved that second act?" he said to the two guys on the couch. "When you have it, let me know. And don't forget, your next project is with me." Before *they* could answer, he was into the dining alcove, leaning over the table of suits. "Yes to a negative pickup," he said. "But you have to give us Europe *and* a completion bond." He picked up an empty pot. "Get these guys some more coffee, Elizabeth." He replaced the pot and shot past them back into his office, closing the door behind him. "Now," he said, "let me tell you the problem we have."

"Let me guess. You've signed a multi-million-dollar deal with a man who's just been arrested for murder."

"Correct."

"And you have to decide whether you want to back him up or not."

"Exactly. But we have to decide quickly because a lot of public relations damage is already done. I'd say in about a week Global Pictures will have to get behind him or let him twist in the wind. I can't imagine he's innocent, but we can't afford to project a bad image on this. It's even more extreme than the Landis case. Try dealing with the talent in this business." He shook his head. "Oh, well, on an assembly line you have to work with asbestos."

"Why me?"

"I saw you at the benefit yesterday. I heard you were working for Emily Ptak."

"Who told you that?"

"Eddy Sandollar."

"How'd he know?"

"Eddy knows everything. It's his business. You might turn out to be a big donor, after all. Anyway, I checked you out. I have facilities to do that in a hurry. So, how much do you get for this?"

"Five hundred a day plus expenses."

"Five hundred? You've been making two hundred."

"You know my fee?"

"That's my job. An agent comes in here asking a hundred thousand for a screenplay, I have to know if that's what the writer's been making."

"Five hundred or forget it."

"All right," he said. "But I was going to offer you another arrangement. Your regular fee and a fifty-thousand-dollar bonus if you solve the case. It's what we call a step deal."

"I'll take it," I said.

When I arrived back, Chantal was sitting in the kitchen reading the paper and drinking coffee.

"Luck is on our side," I said, coming up from behind and kissing her. "We've already got a new client." I told her about Global Pictures and its junior workaholic president. "The only drawback is," I explained, "we've got to get it solved in a week. Otherwise it's of no use to them. Steinway takes us off the payroll. And needless to say, we're never to tell anyone who we're working for."

She pointed to the three-column headline on the front page above photographs of Bannister and Otis: NOTED COMIC HELD IN PSYCHIATRIST SLAYING.

"Anything new in it?"

"They found the corpse exposed in a ravine behind the Serra Retreat. Apparently it was buried under some leaves and slid down."

"That fast? Who found it?"

"Some wranglers at the ranch—Jack Goldman and Danny Aronowitz."

"Kosher cowboys," I said, pouring myself a cup of coffee and slugging down some quick caffeine. "Where was the knife?"

"They don't say. But it was discovered by a Marianne Walders, an aerobics teacher at the Malibu Movers. We'll have to go see her."

"*I'll* do that. I'm going out there to look at the scene of the crime. I want you to stay here and check with Stanley Burckhardt. He's bound to have turned up something by now, and if he hasn't, I'd like to know why. Also, I want to know more about Nastase's trips to Trieste. Get the precise dates and destinations if you can. Where he stayed. Who he saw. Whatever. Check with the INS and see where and when he got his citizenship. There might be something in that. Also, go down to the Hall of Records and find out whether Bannister owned his own house—Sixty-three A, Malibu Colony. It may not tell us much, but it's standard operating procedure. Then meet me at two o'clock at Zucky's Delicatessen on Wilshire.''

"Yes, sir." She looked at me cooly.

"Look, I know what you're thinking. I'd love to spend the whole day with you, do this together, but if we're going to solve this thing, we're going to have to divide and conquer.''

"That wasn't what was bothering me. But anyway ...'' She shrugged, looked away. "When're you going to investigate your shrink?''

"What for?''

"You told me you saw those matches in his office. And that he's Emily's psychiatrist too.''

"Yeah, well, I've been thinking about it. It doesn't make much sense. I mean he can't even get around by himself.''

"You mean he doesn't have a car?''

"He's got this dark green van parked in his driveway. But I don't know how he uses it. I mean, I don't even know if he lives alone.''

Chantal looked at me. When the last words came out, I realized how strange they sounded. In Freudian circles it was conventional thinking for the patient to know little or nothing of his analyst. But those days were long gone, especially in California. So I wondered why I, a private detective, had preferred to remain in the dark. Was there something I didn't want to know? And was it about Nathanson or about me?

Like Montecito and Palos Verdes Estates, Serra Retreat was one of those rare places in Southern California that still reminded you of the dream the world once envied. It felt as if you were in a time warp, driving through a classic orange crate label to a sylvan world as you turned off the Pacific Coast Highway on Cross Creek Road and continued through the gate marked PRIVATE ROAD—PROCEED AT OWN RISK past the perfect little truck farm and the perfect little A-frame with the wooden dolphin statue out front to the creek that was never dry. It was a California Dream for the new gentrified rich, television producers who could smoke their dope in peace in imitation mission-style ranchos so exact, their execution surpassed the originals. Every once in a while they would go out to the corral to see if the Porsche was all right or to readjust the satellite dish.

When I arrived, a number of locals—some kids on skateboards, an aging surfer in a torn wet suit, three Latino maids, and a couple of women by a new Jeep Cherokee not dissimilar to King King's—were standing around the edge of the creek watching a pair of policemen in rubber hip boots trudge back and forth through the mud, probing the scene of the crime with wooden rakes. I parked and ambled up to the surfer in my most laid-back fashion as if I had just lost my way to the Dairy Queen. He had the glazed, brain-damaged look of someone who had had his head bashed by the waves for about thirty years.

"What're they looking for?" I asked, nodding toward the cops. "Escargots?"

"Dude committed suicide."

"He did?"

"He couldn't take it. Women problems."

"Women problems? How do *you* know?"

"It was in the papers. One day he's drinking a bottle of Erlanger's at Enrico's, next day he's offing himself. I met him once. Up at Stinson Beach."

"Stinson Beach. I didn't know he hung out up north. I thought he had his hands full in Malibu."

"Malibu? Dude hated it around here. Too many people. Smog. Traffic. No trout."

"No trout, huh? That *can* be a problem." This one was even further gone than I thought. "Funny," I said. "I read how he was out jogging with that black comic and then he got knifed in the bushes."

"You interested in *that?* A great American poet kills him-self and you're worried about some Mercedes-Benz psychi-atrist?" The surfer turned and looked at me as if I were beneath contempt.

"Trout, huh?" I repeated, suddenly realizing what he was talking about. "*Trout Fishing in America.* Richard Brauti-gan ... the writer. Too bad he committed suicide a year ago."

"Damn straight. A national tragedy." The surfer looked

at me differently now. I had gone up about six notches in his estimation. "No one reads anymore, do they? All they do is watch MTV or rent Cheech and Chong movies at the video store."

"Yeah, well, at least some people go jogging." I nodded toward the creek.

"Narcissists."

"I know what you mean. I bet you read that, too—*The Culture of Narcissism.*"

"Good book," said the surfer.

"Of course, you guys were the original narcissists, getting up at the crack of dawn and paddling out there in that ocean years before the first yuppie came bopping along the beach in his Nike running suit and Reeboks. You must've seen them all come and go."

The surfer nodded. "The long board days," he said, shaking his head nostalgically.

"Did you ever see that shrink running along with the comic?" I gestured toward the cops. One of them had just dredged up a bikini bottom and was showing it to his partner.

"Sometimes. Sometimes I was in the water first."

"What about yesterday?"

The surfer coughed and spat. "Nosy Parker," he said.

"I'm just curious, that's all."

"So are a lot of people." The surfer shrugged, retreating into his wet suit like a turtle into its shell.

I studied him a moment. "Actually I'm a detective novelist," I said. "It's research."

He turned full around and looked at me. "Really? . . . I thought about doing that. Write some books about a surfer detective who works out of his woody in Redondo Beach."

"Sounds like a good angle."

"Wanted to do one about a Beach Boys–type group. The leader, this acid-damaged genius, gets offed and my guy has to find the killer."

"Why don't you do it?"

"Could you help me find an agent?"

"Maybe . . . yeah . . . sure." The surfer grinned, revealing a couple of large gaps in his teeth where he must have been reamed by his board. "What *about* yesterday?" I continued. "Did you see them jogging?"

"Sure did."

"Notice anything exceptional? . . . It's good practice. For writing."

"Yeah. That Otis dude was really dogging it. Looked like he hadn't slept all night. The shrink kept being pissed off because he wouldn't keep up. Then something funny happened. Someone came up and asked Otis for his autograph."

"Why's that funny?"

"Around Malibu Colony Beach? They got everybody jogging out here in the morning—Dyan Cannon, Shirley MacLaine. It's like goddamned *People* magazine. Nobody asks for an autograph. It's just not cool. You know what I mean?"

"Yeah. So who stopped him?"

"Some dude. Maybe around thirty. Dark hair. I didn't get a good look at him 'cause I was hurryin' to untie my board. They were breaking about four feet at the time. Anyway, he comes up just as Otis is about to cross the PCH down at the other end of Serra Retreat. The shrink's already on the other side treading water while Otis signs and the light changes and the dude is stuck there.''

"Which dude? Otis or the shrink?"

"Both of 'em. So the shrink gets impatient and starts off ahead of him into the other end of the Retreat where those big stone pillars are.''

"So he could've been killed right there.''

"Whaddaya mean? His body was over here." He pointed to the creek where the cop had now found the bikini top and was now teasingly offering the matched set to the ladies with the Jeep. "It rolled down that hill.''

"You mean that's where they *found* it. Actually, he could've been killed behind those isolated pillars and then dragged over here without Otis ever knowing about it.''

"Yeah," said the surfer, eyeing me carefully. "That's interesting. I can see why you're a detective writer. What's your name?"

"Robert Parker," I said.

"Hey. No shit?" He looked amazed. "I read some of your stuff. You're good.''

Ten minutes later I was with Marianne Walders, the aerobics instructor at the Malibu Movers who had discovered the murder weapon. She had the kind of body generally associated with her trade and I was staring at her sweatshirt, which said Movers Shake It Better, in order to concentrate on my role as an Auto Club investigator. It was one of my favorite parts of detective work, playing a role or what was called in the trade "running a gag" to get information. Nathanson said I liked it so much because it was a disguised act of aggression. But at the moment, everything Nathanson had told me had been called into question.

"As you know, the Auto Club doesn't just come out and change your tire on a dark night. We're a full service company—emergency road service, travel, *and* insurance," I told Marianne, who was standing behind the counter in the tight entry room, a couple of matrons visible in the mirror behind her, doing a feeble can-can to a Tina Turner album.

"Yes, I know," she said, smiling pleasantly. It had been my experience that the Auto Club was the most successful of "gags." Everybody, even the congenitally paranoid and disgruntled, trusted the Auto Club.

"So a claim has already been made on behalf of this Dr. Bannister and we want to get it processed as quickly as possible. Can you tell me anything about him?"

"I never met the man."

"I see. And what about Otis King?"

"Him neither. Although I've seen him on TV. He's funny. I never could understand why he stuck with that partner." Then she winced, suddenly realizing: "Oh, he's the one who committed suicide, isn't he?"

"I believe so. What about the murder weapon? We have a report that it was found on the premises."

"Well, not exactly *on* the premises. Come. I'll show you."

I followed her outside onto a balcony that overlooked the back of the small, two-story office building that contained the Movers, a surfboard rental, a video rental, a windsurfing rental, a jet ski rental, and a frozen yogurt shop—all those marginal outfits that seemed to stay in operation just for the dubious distinction of doing business in Malibu. They were all backed up against the hill exactly where the road ran off the Coast Highway into the Serra Retreat.

"The knife was hidden behind there. Right where they leave the boxes."

"What boxes?"

"The Evian water. Every Monday, Wednesday, and Friday night the liquor store guy leaves two cartons of Evian by our door. I pick them up the next morning."

"And this is a regular habit?"

"Hey, after a good workout no one wants to drink tap water." She made a face. "It would ruin everything."

16

"Wait a minute. Wait a minute. Run this by me again. Nathanson was Bannister's teacher?"

"And advisor. At the Southern California School of Psychotherapy. In fact, Nathanson edited a book in which Bannister was one of the principal contributors: *Aspects of the Psychodynamic Method.*"

"Where'd you find this out?" We were sitting at Zucky's with the menus in our hands, but I was rapidly losing my appetite.

"At the *Times.*"

"At the *Times*? What were you doing there?" My irritated voice carried over to the next table, where a geriatric couple looked up from their stuffed derma.

"We're not going to get much help from the police," said Chantal, lowering her voice pointedly, "so I figured I ought to make friends with the newspaper people covering the case. The guy writing the obituary had it with his background information."

"You can't do this. I have to know where you are at all times." I knew I was sounding like an asshole, but I couldn't stop myself. This Nathanson business was turning me into a jerk.

"Why?"

"Coordination. It's ... it's absolutely necessary."

"So I'm not to use my initiative."

"I didn't say that."

"What *are* you saying?"

I brooded for a moment. "Where's Burckhardt?"

"I don't know. I couldn't find him."

"See? That was your first responsibility."

"Good-bye." She got up and started walking out of the restaurant.

"Wait a minute—" I got up and started after her. "Where're you going?"

"I'm leaving."

"Leaving? ... What—"

"If this is the kind of partnership we're going to have, it's not worth it. There are other things I can do."

"Like what?" I stepped into her path. The old people with the stuffed derma were having quite a show.

"Well, for example, the California Institute of Hypnotherapy can get you a therapist's license in six months."

"*You* want to be a therapist?"

"What's wrong with that?"

"You're too neurotic to—"

"Okay. That's it." She started around me at a brisk clip.

"Wait, wait. I'm sorry. You're right." She slowed. "I was being defensive. I guess I don't want to hear"—I lowered my voice—"weird things about Nathanson. But one thing: you can't go running off at the drop of a hat. This is a tough business and that kind of behavior doesn't inspire confidence."

She stood there watching me like a wary animal.

"He canceled," she said.

"What?"

"Nathanson canceled your next appointment. It was on your answering machine."

"Did he say why?"

"No."

"That's strange. Oh, well," I said, sounding a lot calmer than I felt. In fact, my heart was in my throat. "I guess, then, we'll have to check him out." I glanced at my watch. "But we still have time to get something to eat and be there at ten of three. Nothing much interesting happens at a shrink's office until five minutes before the hour anyway."

I waited for Chantal to react, but she continued to stand there. "I forgot to tell you something else," she said at length.

"What?"

"I went down to the Hall of Records. Bannister didn't own his house. It belongs to VIP Leasing of the Grand Bahamas."

"Tax havens," I said. "God knows who that is. Maybe it's even Bannister himself, recycling a little of his celebrity cash."

At five minutes before three we were sitting in Chantal's rented car at an intersection a half block away from Nathanson's house. A maroon Peugeot was parked out front, probably a patient's; the green van was parked in the back. We didn't say anything, watching the digital seconds tick off on the dashboard clock. At approximately two minutes to the hour, a woman with dirty blond hair emerged, got into the Peugeot, and drove off. Almost on cue, a blue Volvo wagon drove up and a woman of about sixty got out and entered the house. Chantal wrote her description and license plate number on a note pad. I shifted in my seat. I was feeling uncomfortable, as if I were doing something that wasn't quite right, like spying on a parent.

Nothing happened for the next twenty minutes. I turned to Chantal.

"This is surveillance," I said. "You can't read and you can't sleep and it can go on for days like this. Pretty glamorous, huh?"

"I find it interesting."

"Really? Tell me in about a year."

I took advantage of her presence, closed my eyes, and pushed the seat back. In a few minutes I had gone off to sleep. I didn't notice a thing until I felt Chantal elbowing me in the ribs. It was eight minutes to four and the older woman was exiting from Nathanson's and crossing to her Volvo. She was a stout woman and her face betrayed no emotion. Over the course of months I had experienced a variety of reactions and I wondered how *she* felt, coming out of her sessions. Was she angry, depressed, elated? Did she think it was worth the money? Or was she so rich it didn't matter?

I didn't have much time to cogitate on this because barely had the Volvo driven off when a side door to Nathanson's house I had never noticed swung open and a beefy black-haired man in a white surgical coat emerged, walking slowly backward. He was balancing Nathanson himself on his wheelchair, easing him down a ramp onto the blacktop drive-way. He turned the psychiatrist around, pushed him toward the van, and stopped, opening the doors and lifting him onto the front passenger seat. Then the orderly shut the passenger door, got into the driver's seat, and headed off. I slumped low like a disobedient child as he drove past within five feet of our car.

I waited for them to make a left at the intersection, then made a U-turn and followed. What was I doing? I wondered. Was this idle curiosity? So what if he canceled a session? That wasn't so extraordinary. What did I expect? That he would get on the freeway and head downtown for another hotel tryst with Emily Ptak? And how could this relate to the epidemic of murder and/or suicide that had struck Malibu and points east the last few weeks? Probably he was just going to the store, off to park in one of those handicapped zones that were always infuriatingly empty in the busiest of shopping center lots. Whatever it was, it was probably a

delay of game in the ever-urgent eyes of the likes of Nick
Steinway anyway.

I followed him up Entrada to Ocean Avenue, where he
continued along the Santa Monica Palisade, its Old World
graciousness teetering precariously on the imminent threat
of a Pacific slide. He turned on Colorado, then again on
Fourth, making a left onto the Santa Monica Freeway and
heading downtown. Maybe he *was* going to the Bonaventure.

I stayed two cars behind as the van sped under the San
Diego Freeway, passing the off ramps at Overland, Robert-
son, La Cienega, and La Brea. Just as the Bonaventure was
visible in the distance, its silver-mirrored tubes looming like
designer missile silos against the darkening sky, he veered
off at the Crenshaw ramp, heading north toward the hills.
We crossed Pico and the signs started changing from English to Asian, the shopping centers from flat-roofed Middle
American to blue-tiled, ersatz Oriental with funny little pa-
godas sprouting from traditional California stucco. We were
in Koreatown, the fastest-growing neighborhood in Los Angeles, so fast-growing, in fact, that it seemed to double in
size every few weeks; but not in the charming ragtag manner
of the Chinese or the aesthetic Zen-orderliness of the Japanese, but in the simple land-devouring eagerness of typical
American materialism. In more ways than one, the Koreans
were our Seoul brothers.

Nathanson pulled to one of the larger shopping centers
and parked, in the handicapped zone, in front of a huge
garishly painted restaurant called the New Inchon. I stopped
across the street and waited as his bearlike driver emerged,
withdrew the wheelchair, opened it, and carefully deposited

the psychiatrist on the seat. Then, after making sure Nathanson's feet were properly situated in the loop of the footplate and releasing the wheel lock, he guided the doctor up a ramp and through the carved wooden door of the restaurant.

"Okay. I admit it," said Chantal. "We're wasting our time. He's just gone out for dinner."

"Possibly. But let's see."

I nodded to her and she followed me out of the car. We crossed the lot to the restaurant and I opened the door slowly, making certain we didn't run straight into Nathanson on the other side.

I was confronted by a wall-size map of a mythically unified Korea beneath a portrait of the South's present leader, General Chun Doo Hwan. I stepped in, motioning for Chantal. We stood in the entry room, looking past a bronze Buddha into the restaurant itself. It was well lit and noisy, divided into a series of rooms for sushi, tempura, and Korean-style barbecue called bul-go-kee that was cooked at tables on individual grills. I searched through the crowd, which was almost entirely Korean, well-dressed bourgeois types who, except for their Mongoloid faces, could have been from the Valley or the Marina. Some of the men even wore the requisite open-throated shirts with gold chains. Their women were similarly clad in expensive fashions, ready for a night out in a determinedly upwardly mobile society. The food smelled good and I had half a mind to sit and sample some myself when I noticed Nathanson, two rooms off, being pushed through a doorway that, it seemed, led out the back of the restaurant. A tall, lean Korean in a leisure suit was showing the way for the driver.

We waited a couple of minutes, then, ignoring the maître
d' who was trying to seat us, continued after them. The
doorway gave onto a corridor that led past the kitchen. We
walked along, doing our best not to answer the curious stares
of the cooks and dishwashers, to a fire door. I pushed
through it into an alley just behind a Dempster Dumpster.
Chantal joined me, and we looked down to the end of the
alley, which was blocked by a graphite Mercedes limousine.
Nathanson, still in his wheelchair, was facing the rear of the
limo, where a gray-haired Korean in a blue suit was sitting
with the window opened. I could hear them talking to each
other, but I couldn't distinguish the words. I was about to
move closer, when I heard the sharp flick of a blade.

"Hey, smart dog, we meet again."

It was the Chu's Brothers.

With all their knives and chains.

"Get inside," I yelled to Chantal. She didn't move. "I
said *get inside.*" She still didn't move. She was frozen.

"What ya doin' here, smart dog? Come to see the Reverend?" He started backing us toward the dumpster while
his partner edged between us and the door.

"Reverend?"

"Don't play dumb with me, smart dog. I know why you're
here. Jesus Saves, right?"

"Right."

"And talk in tongues. I know you can talk in tongues,
right, smart dog?"

"Sure." I looked over from the two Chu's to Chantal.
Down at the end of the alley I could hear the sound of a
motor turning over.

"Do it," he said.

"Do what?"

"Talk in tongues. I wanna hear you talk in tongues. You're a religious person. You're here to see the Reverend, get his advice and counsel. *Talk!*"

He moved toward me, grinning and pushing upward with his knife. A door slammed. I glanced down the alley. Nathanson was being loaded into the limousine next to the gray-haired Korean.

"What's the matter, smart dog? Cat got your tongue? Can't speak in tongues and the cat's got your tongue. I think they're Satanists, Brother Chu. I think they're on the *wrong side!*"

The silent Chu pulled a chain from under his leather jacket and started advancing on Chantal.

"I can speak tongues," she blurted suddenly, clasping her hands in front of her and talking a mile a minute. "I'm a Catholic girl. Raised in a convent. In Quebec. By nuns. Strict nuns. And mean Jesuits. With rulers. Made us pray every fifteen minutes. On our knees. Father, Son, and the Holy Ghost. Jesus, Mary, and Joseph. Matthew, Mark, Luke, and John. Body and blood. Holy Communion. Feel the stigmata. Feel the presence. Mary, Mary, full of grace."

"That's not *tongues.* This girl's bullshittin' us, isn't she, Brother Chu? That's sacrilege! Get that sister of Satan!"

The silent Chu started whipping the air with his chain, swirling it within inches of Chantal.

"Help! Help, police!" she screamed.

The Chu's whirled around. I kicked the verbal Chu in the stomach, stunning him just long enough to chop his partner in the neck and grab Chantal, pulling her back into the restaurant.

"Holy Mother of ..." she shouted and ran like a gazelle down the restaurant corridor, nearly knocking over some busboys and a patron waiting to use the pay phone. I slammed through the front door after her and dashed across the parking lot. She didn't say another word until we had reached the car, I had locked all four doors, and we were out of the parking lot.

"I quit," she said. "I can't do *this*. I'm a coward. I'm afraid of flying. I'm afraid of the dark. I'm afraid of snakes. I'm afraid of goddamned spiders. What the hell do I want to be a detective for?"

"That's a good question." I was driving around the block, looking for the graphite limousine, but there was no sign of it. "Actually, you didn't do too badly under the circumstances. You kept your cool."

"Yeah, but right now I feel like I'm ready for the intensive care unit ... I'll need a gun," she said.

"A gun?"

"We're gonna deal with creeps like that, I'm gonna need a gun. For self-defense. A thirty-eight."

"A thirty-eight will take your arm off. You'll be feeling the recoil for a month. Besides, most people can't hit an elephant at five yards with a gun like that."

"Then I'll get one of those little derringers like Miss Kitty had on *Gunsmoke*. And I'll go out for target practice every morning until I can hit all the tin cans off the garden fence. Who *were* those guys?"

"The Chu's Brothers."

"Them again. What were *they* doing around here with Nathanson and that warlord in the limo? Is *he* the Reverend? And what was *that* about? I feel like I'm in the middle of an episode of *Terry and the Pirates.* Are those guys punkers or Jesus freaks or what?"

"Beats me," I said. She was starting to smile now, in spite of herself. "Maybe they're born-again bikers. B again B— just like Nastase's thing."

"Wasn't that B *for* B?"

"Right. B for B. Brains for billions. Beans for Boston ... Wait a minute—Bibles. There were boxes of Bibles in Nastase's house. Boxes for Bibles. That doesn't make much sense."

"How about Bibles for Billy? He's an undercover agent for Billy Graham."

"Or *Bibles for Bonzo.* It's a remake of the old Reagan movie."

"That's it," said Chantal, grinning. "The crazy chimp starts ripping pages out of Deuteronomy until Nancy gets wind of him and locks him up with Mike Deaver and Betsy Bloomingdale at the Santa Barbara ranch. ... Wait a minute. Where are we?"

"Santa Monica and Western."

She checked her watch. "I've got to be at the Fun Zone in five minutes."

"The Fun Zone?"

"Yeah. I'm on tonight at nine-thirty and twelve. I've got to be in makeup. If you don't mind dropping me off, I'll ..." She stopped, noticing my expression. "Hey, look, we're not exactly Interpol yet and entertainment *is* my business."

"Is this your idea of partnership? We're in the middle of a case here."

"Hey, I know. But a girl's gotta keep all her balls in the air. You don't expect me to give up my shot at the Carson show for a little cops and robbers. I mean it's not interfering or anything. And I won't stop thinking about it for a second. I promise."

"Uh-huh."

There was an uncomfortable silence as I hit the freeway, getting off at Highland and jogging over Sunset to the Fun Zone. I dropped her off at the club with a quick peck on the cheek.

"See you later," she said. "And don't worry. We'll lick this thing." She ran straight to the stage door without looking back.

I sat there a moment, staring over at the Albergo Picasso, the image of Ptak flying over the penthouse wall describing a parabola in my mind. It seemed less and less like suicide, but who had pushed him over? Not Nastase, that was clear. More likely someone who had been using the poor slob and thought nothing of removing him the minute things got hot, someone bloodless enough to send that contra retread chasing me all over New York. I sure hoped it wasn't Nathanson.

I started to pull out of the Fun Zone lot when I heard a tap on my rear windshield. It was Koontz. He walked around and let himself into the passenger side without waiting for an invitation.

"Well, well, Art Koontz, comedy's friend. Can't keep this man away from the yucks. You ought to try the Catskills on your next vacation."

"Actually, I just stopped by on my way back from the Learning League. I'm taking this terrific course in integrated business software. You should try it. It's—"

"Save it, Koontz."

"All right. All right. But don't say I never gave you any sound advice. Maybe you'd listen if I were that fancy headshrinker of yours."

"At the moment, I doubt it."

"Well, that's an improvement. Anyway, I'm glad I saw you, because it's going to save me a phone call. If you continue to muck around in the King case, I'm going to have to get a restraining order."

"You're what?"

"Look, it's nothing personal, but this isn't a situation for the little guy. Everybody's in it now—the FBI, the DEA. They issued another warrant this morning."

"For whom?"

"King King. According to the U.S. Attorney's office, thanks to information *we* brought them, he's nailed up the giggy. But you know what? He wasn't there. As of yesterday, just about the time his brother butchered Bannister, the great, impregnable King King flew the coop. Remarkable coincidence, isn't it?"

"Any leads?"

"Leads? He's probably down on Copacabana Beach fucking little girls until his pecker falls off. Great justice, huh? Or do you sympathize with him, too, just because *he's* black."

"Ease off, Koontz."

"The DEA's going up the wall. Ten fucking years they've

been trying to get that scumbag. Ten fucking years! They find you mucking around in this, they'll hang us both out to dry before they even know your name. So, my old friend"— he tapped me on the arm—"I'm serious about that restraining order. Stay out of this one. In fact, do yourself a favor and get out of this racket altogether. You're a bright boy. This is the eighties. Most of your old comrades are running corporations by now. Think positively. Think—"

"Don't tell me. Integrated business software."

"Right," he said. And got out of the car.

I made a U-turn for his edification, as if I were heading home, but then doubled back a few blocks off to pay a surprise visit to Emily Ptak. Cars were in the driveway and the lights were on when I arrived at the Tudor estate at the end of West Wanda. I parked in front of the guard gate and pressed the intercom button. I was answered in a few seconds by the voice of the nanny as, simultaneously, I saw a video camera go into surveillance mode. Life in the big city.

"May we help you?"

"Yes. My name is Moses Wine. I used to work with Mrs. Ptak. I know it's late, but it's very important that I ask her a few questions."

"One moment, please."

I stood there a few minutes, staring into the darkness before the voice came back on.

"I'm sorry. Mrs. Ptak is reading her daughter a story and does not wish to be disturbed."

"Tell her I'll wait."

"I don't think that would be advisable, Mr. Wine."

"Tell her there are some problems to resolve regarding

her visit to the Bonaventure Hotel the day before yesterday."

The intercom went silent again. After a longer wait, the gate opened. I got back into my car and drove through, pulling in behind an Audi diesel that looked about two months old. Emily was waiting at the door when I got out. She was wearing a maroon housecoat with gray piping and she looked tired.

"Hello," she said, her voice as cool as dry ice as she led me inside, making a quick left turn into a pine-paneled den that was right off the foyer. The room was lined with books and framed memorabilia from the career of her deceased husband. She shut the door and pointed to a leather armchair. "Let's make this brief. As far as I'm concerned, we have nothing left to say to each other."

"We never said much in the first place. Emily, how was your relationship with your husband?"

"Ambivalent. Ambivalence is the natural condition of the state of matrimony. Surely you're old enough to know that."

"Maybe, but I'm a romantic."

"What exactly do you want, Mr. Wine?"

"Who was the man with you in Room Seven-fifteen of the Bonaventure?"

"That's my business."

"Emily, several capital crimes have been committed here. Sooner or later there are going to be grand jury investigations, trials. You're certain to be subpoenaed."

"My private life at the Bonaventure or anywhere else has nothing whatsoever to do with any crime. Or is there a law against having a libido in this blue-stocking society?"

"It's only curious that less than two weeks after the death of your husband, you're having a hotel tryst with another man. I would assume this was going on before he died."

"And?"

"And some ninety percent of murders take place within the family."

"Among people who are ruled by their emotions. I've spent five years and an embarrassing amount of money in this obscenely privileged society of ours to make sure I am not. Besides, I'm sure you're aware that we're all capable of loving more than one person at a time. Sometimes with equal intensity. Our children teach us that. It's just that some of us deny ourselves that joy."

"You learned that in therapy, no doubt."

"Among many other things."

"Then if you've got this all so rationalized, I don't understand why you had any objection to seeing me tonight."

"This whole episode is becoming more and more bizarre and violent. Lurid. Right out of the *National Enquirer*. The one great problem Mike and I always had was I hated the public life, hated the exhibitionism. That probably drove us apart more than anything. Right now it's driving me crazy. I can't stand it. I don't want to hear any more about this. I don't want to think about it. I don't want to see anyone connected with it. I just want to do my best to forget the whole thing, hard as that may be, and disappear."

"Then no more fancy benefits with Eddy Sandollar."

"I resent that, Mr. Wine. Those benefits exist for a greater good. Not for anybody's personal aggrandizement."

"And you'll keep your affair buried forever?"

"That affair is over. It ended that very day at the Bonaventure. And I can assure you, it has no chance of rekindling. Now, if you'll excuse me, I want to go back to reading my daughter *Babar.*" She went and opened the door for me.

"Can you answer one last question?"

"That depends."

"Did you ever have sexual relations with Eugene Nathanson?"

"There's no way I'd answer that. I believe the therapist-patient relationship is the most sacred bond in our society."

"Yeah. I wouldn't doubt you do." I started out. "Did Mike know about your affair?"

"Yes. Of course. We were married since we were twenty. He knew everything I did and I knew everything he did, even when he tried to hide it. I knew about his insecurities, the girls he fucked, his drugs, his debts, his self-destructiveness. He pissed it all away joylessly because he didn't think he deserved anything. There wasn't a penny left in his estate. Look it up in your records, Mr. Detective. The only thing he left me was this house. And even that's not worth much. It's on a fault."

"Then why were you so sure he didn't commit suicide?"

"He wouldn't have had the guts. Good night."

She closed the door in my face, leaving me standing there in the afterglow of her bitterness.

I was still feeling it when I unlocked the door of my apartment twenty minutes later. I went into my bedroom and played my messages. A private eye in Detroit wanted to know if I'd help him do a skip trace on a deadbeat named Jack Luchese. My son Jacob needed forty dollars for his Columbia applica-

tion, and Nick Steinway called to ask how it was going and to
say they were sending over something called a "deal memo"
to sign concerning my short-term employment with Global Pictures. I could call him at his office tomorrow any time after
five A.M. but not after six-thirty, because that's when he went
into a staff meeting and then went off to London, Paris, and
Tunisia and wouldn't be back in L.A. for thirty-six hours. This
guy made Sammy Glick seem like Krishnamurti.

I sank down on the bed and pulled a joint out of the end
table drawer. I was about to go into the kitchen for a match,
but fumbling in my pocket, I found a book. I started to light
the joint, when I noticed its jacket had a hand reaching out
toward you with the words I WAS THERE—COMEDIANS &
CHEFS BENEFIT FOR AFRICA/24-HOUR RELIEF HOT LINE—
1-800-234-HELP. I lit my joint and dialed the number. It rang
once before picking up with a recording of a now familiar
voice. I could hear what sounded like tribal drumming behind him as he spoke: "This is Eddy Sandollar talking to
you live from Harar, Ethiopia. As I speak, rains have be-
gun to fall, giving some respite to this benighted land. But
do not be misled by falsely optimistic reports in the press.
This is only a temporary lull in an ongoing struggle of
mammoth proportions. We need nothing less than a Mar-
shall Plan for Africa. It's our planetary responsibility.
Whether you pray to Buddha, Jesus, Yahweh, or the Spirit
in the Sky, I know you will want to join me on this crusade
against world hunger. At the sound of the beep, leave your
name, number, and the time that you called, and one of
our volunteers will contact you for your pledge the next
working day. *Namaste.*"

Beep.

"This is Moses Wine, 555-4273. Tell Mr. Sandollar to call me."

I hung up and lay back on the bed, stopping first to punch "play" on my video deck. *The Best of Mike Ptak* was still in the machine, and the dead comic doing a George Bush imitation flickered onto the screen. I didn't know who was more boring—the original or the copy. But the net result was the same as my last attempt to study Ptak's work: within five minutes I went crashing off to sleep.

"Wake up! Wake up! I've got it!" said a voice, dimly piercing through my dream state. I forced my eyes open to see Chantal bursting with excitement, pacing at the end of my bed. It was just past two A.M. "I figured it out. Boy, was I brilliant. I mean, I usually don't toot my own horn, but tonight I killed them. They were on the floor. Stella Resnick's thinking about putting me in for a solo. Screw that esoteric Franco-Canuck garbage. This is the real thing, a *unique act*—comedienne/private eye. By day you're a bloodhound on the case and by night you describe all the weirdos you met while you were doing it. It knocked their socks off."

"It *what?*" By now I was sitting up in my bed with my eyes wide open.

"Hey, what're you so excited about? I told you I figured it out—B for B. It just came out of my mouth while I was free-associating. That's how it happens in stand-up. When you're cooking, things just pop out."

"Now wait just one second. You're telling me you were standing in front of a public audience at the Fun Zone giving intimate details of our investigation?"

"Well, not in any particular order. I mean, I don't think they could possibly—"

"Who the hell do you think you are? That's the most unprofessional thing I've *ever* heard! You have *no idea* who was out there."

"You have no right to tell me what to do."

"But I do! You work for me and your behavior is ridiculous. You can't go around—"

"I didn't give away *anything.*"

"How do you know?"

"How do I know? I was the one who was there ... oh, the hell with it." She went into the bathroom and grabbed her things, muttering as she came out again. "I was right in the first place. Mixing business and private life makes a mess of everything. So I think for both of our sakes we should just break it all off right here."

"What?"

"I'm leaving."

"I didn't ask you to do that."

"I'm not a charity case and if you don't trust the way I do things, as far as I'm concerned, there's no point. So good-bye."

"Good-bye."

She started out of my bedroom, then stopped for a moment by the door. "Oh, as you may recall, Nastase was a Romanian. So it should be obvious: B for B is Bibles for Bucharest."

She closed the door and left.

17

When I tried Chantal the next morning, the phone was off the hook. Later on, I got a machine. Fuck it, I thought. We're all neurotics. It's hopeless. And I went into the shower.

I had just finished drying myself when Koontz called.

"Your girl friend put on quite a show last night."

"She's not my girl friend now."

"Oh, yeah? That's interesting. The way she was describing you on stage, she made you sound like a combination of Humphrey Bogart and John the Twenty-third. But that's none of my business. Anyway, she *did* put the icing on that restraining order. It should be in place in about fifteen minutes. Sorry about that. Look, I know this sounds like the Lonely Guys Club, but if you aren't doing anything Thursday night, that integrated software class—"

"Thanks, but no thanks."

"Don't mention it."

He hung up just in time for the doorbell to ring. It was the messenger for Global Pictures with the deal memo.

"Mr. Steinway wants me to wait while you sign this."

"My lawyer likes to see these things first." I said, opening the envelope. I could just see myself being dragged into court by a bull terrier like Steinway over a noncompliance issue.

"I'm not supposed to leave without it," he said, handing me a pen. He planted himself inside the doorway as if he were a process server for the IRS. I would be the one needing a restraining order to get *him* out.

"Look, this isn't—" I started to say, when the phone rang. "Hello."

A voice whispered: "The money is moving."

"What?"

"The money is moving."

"Who is this?"

"A Christian."

"A Christian. Great. Look, hold on a second here." I turned to the messenger. "All right. All right. Here. Take it." I scrawled my signature on the bottom line of the memo and handed it to him. "Now, if you'll excuse me, this is a—"

"You didn't date it," he said.

I quickly wrote out the date and handed it back to him. The messenger nodded and left.

"Hello, Mr. Christian."

Silence.

"Hello."

"Look for the medicine."

"Medicine? What medicine?"

No response.

"Hello? ... Hello?...."

A click.

Christian. Medicine. Bibles for Bucharest. Burckhardt, I thought. Two minutes later I was in my car, heading down

La Cienega toward the Miracle Mile. It was raining hard, the first rain of the year, and cars were skidding all over the place from the fresh road oils. L.A. drivers never remember how to drive in wet weather from one year to the next, and it was like a game of bumper cars all the way to the dismal facade of the Fallbrook Arms.

I climbed the stairs quickly with the sudden urgency of a man who is afraid of the inevitable. This increased when I found Burckhardt's door locked. I banged on it a few times and then, smiling at the Chicano delivery boys who were loitering in the corridor, let myself in with my lockpicks. The way they didn't bat an eyelash, they were probably there for the same thing.

No one was in the office. Much to my relief no one was in the bathroom or the closet either. Of course, he could have been off in the woods someplace. Or at the bottom of a garbage heap. Burckhardt was the kind of guy who could have been dead for five years and no one would ever have known it.

I rummaged around in his desk for a while, finding nothing but some unpaid utility bills and an amazing collection of candy bar wrappers. Then I sat down and borrowed his phone. Luckily, it was still connected. I called information for the number of Cosmic Aid headquarters in Ojai and dialed them.

"Eddy Sandollar, please," I said.

"Mr. Sandollar isn't here at the moment," said the receptionist. "Is there someone else who could help you?"

"I'd like to speak with Mr. Sandollar directly. This is kind of an emergency. Is there somewhere I can reach him?"

"Does he know you?"

"Yes, he does. My name is Moses Wine."

"Hold the line, please."

In a few minutes she was back on the line asking for my number. Eddy would call me directly. I hung up and the line rang inside of a minute.

"Hello, Moses."

"Hi, Eddy. Thanks for calling."

"No problem. God, that was some zoo the other day. I don't think I'll ever forget it."

"I don't think any of us will. Look, Eddy, are you still in L.A.? Because I think you could help me figure out a few things."

"Jeez, Moses, I'd like to help you, but I'm on my way back to Ojai in half an hour. I'm going to Ethiopia in three days to supervise the delivery of some Land-Rovers. If you don't do it yourself, they'll use them to invade the Sudan or something. You know how it is over there—the poorer the country, the bigger the army."

"So I heard. Where are you right now? Maybe we could meet for just a few minutes. It's very important."

"Sure, Moses. Sure. You know Ben Franks on Sunset? Meet me there in fifteen minutes."

Sandollar was sitting at a table in Ben Franks with his head buried in *Billboard* when I got there.

"Still reading the old bible," I said, sitting down opposite him. He didn't look as if he had slept much the last couple of nights. I could hardly blame him.

"It's a hard habit to break. Got any suggestions?"

"No. Is there anything wrong with it?"

"I don't know. It feels like an addiction. And I've got more important things to do with my life now than worry about which group is number one with a bullet."

"I guess you do. But speaking of Bibles, ever hear of an organization called Bibles for Bucharest?"

"Bibles for Bucharest?" He laughed. "As in Romania?" He rolled up the *Billboard* and tapped it on the table. "Sounds like one of those old organizations that used to smuggle Bibles behind the Iron Curtain. I think there was a guy once who made millions that way."

"Millions?"

"You get an eight-hundred number, get on one of those cable networks, and say you're going to bring God to the atheists. It starts rolling in so fast you can't count it."

"What about a Korean reverend? Would he have had anything to do with that?"

"I wouldn't know." He smiled. "There's always Reverend Moon."

"Anyone less well known than that?"

"Probably. The Koreans are very evangelically minded. What's all this about?"

"I'm not sure. But somehow I think it relates to the deaths of Mike Ptak, Vasile Nastase, and probably Carl Bannister."

"Well, that's interesting. I hope you're right. I sure hope Otis and his brother aren't responsible."

"How would I find out about a Korean reverend?"

"Well, I'm not exactly sure. That isn't really my line. Cosmic Aid tries to keep a nonsectarian profile. Besides, these religious organizations are pretty well protected. The government can't even get into their books. It's really quite a scandal. I've heard a lot of stories."

"Like what?"

"Relief organizations collecting small fortunes and then sticking them in the bank and living off the interest. Or using them to build multi-zillion-dollar headquarters to rival small corporations. Hell, even Live Aid didn't know how to spend its money. They had millions in the bank for over a year before ... But, hey, Moses, look, I wish I could help you some more, but like I said, I do have to get back. Good luck with this, huh? And keep me posted. If there's anything I can do to help Otis, it'd mean a lot to me." He stood. "And, frankly, it doesn't look so great for Cosmic Aid, if you know what I mean. That wasn't our most successful fund raiser. Check you later." He shook my hand and started out.

"One last quick one."

"Sure."

"What about medicine? Are there any scams to do with medicine?"

"Why not?"

"Bad medicine?"

"Not bad. Outdated. You know the drug companies. The world's biggest overproducers. They've got to get rid of the stuff somehow."

"So they sell it to relief organizations at a discount."

"You got it."

"And the charity pockets the difference."

"Makes everybody happy, doesn't it?" He checked his watch. "Now I've really got to go." He suddenly noticed the

Billboard stashed under his arm and handed it to me.
"You'd better keep this. Bad karma, you know. 'Bye." And
he was out.

Christians, Bibles, and outdated medicines. I sat there
rolling over that Holy Trinity and wondering if they connected in some way to Ptak and his so-called twenty-five
million. That was a lot of aspirins, even at today's inflated
rates. But then, Elmer Gantry never had cable access.

Five minutes later I was on the road myself, heading
downtown. Given the restraining order, I would have to pass
up Otis's bail hearing, but there was nothing to stop me
from checking the fictitious business names index for Bibles
for Bucharest. And also for something like "nestor" or "nestron," the word, according to Chantal, Mike Ptak had bel-
lowed from the penthouse of the Albergo Picasso as he
plummeted to his death. And if that index happened to be
in the civil court building on Hill Street, only just around
the corner from the criminal courts on Temple, well, I had
no control over that.

But I hadn't gone more than half a mile when I picked
up a blue Dodge in my rearview mirror. Its driver was the
same Scott Glenn look-alike who had been pursuing me all
over New York. In the eighties, I thought, even the killers
were bicoastal. I didn't waste any time. I pulled into the
parking lot of a Burger King, walked over to the most public
pay phone I could find, dropped in a quarter, and dialed.

"Parker Center," came the voice on the other end.

"Commander Koontz, please."

"Line's busy. Can you hold?"

"No. Get me John Lu at the Asian Squad."

The phone rang. "Lu here."

"Hello, John. Moses Wine."

There was a slight pause. I looked down the street for my New York friend but couldn't see him. "Hello, Moses." Lu sounded about as happy to hear from me as a physician from a malpractice attorney.

"Listen, uh, John, could you answer a small question for me? It's about those Chu's Brothers. They seem to be adherents of some rev—"

"Sorry, Moses. I'm not supposed to talk to you."

"I see. But this is—"

"I can't."

"All right. That's the way it is, huh? Get me Koontz."

"I'll try."

This time the line was free.

"Koontz here."

"Wine here."

"What now?"

"I'm being followed."

"What're you doing *out*?"

"I'm serious, Koontz. You've got to lift that restraining order. I'm being followed by a hired killer from New York."

"That's not surprising at all. This is a DEA case. Now get inside where the guy can't shoot you, shut your door, and don't open it. Or do I have to put you under arrest? Didn't you read the papers this morning? There's massive evidence of continued rise in coke use in this city. Everybody's embarrassed and the commissioner's trying to run for mayor. Somebody's going to take the heat for it and I don't want it to be me."

"Look, you guys don't have the right line on this case. There's something very different going on."

"Dream on, white boy."

"I'm not sure what exactly, but it has something to do with a giant rip-off in the world of international aid or Christian relief."

"Do you have any evidence of this?"

"No, but—"

"Look, Wine, let me be frank with you. Ever since you've been seeing that psychiatrist of yours, I think you've been going a little bit off."

"That's the problem. He's one of the people I suspect."

"See what I mean? I don't consider myself an expert, but I took a shrink course at the academy and I know they call that acute paranoia. Go home."

He hung up.

I looked down the street for the New Yorker, but I still didn't see him. I got back in my car and drove slowly downtown. I wasn't feeling comfortable. In fact, I was feeling as lonely and alienated as I had ever been. I didn't have a real case, I didn't have a partner, and what client I had would undoubtedly renege when he found I was legally incapable of performing my duties. It was the pathetic summation of fifteen years of private investigative work. Mean streets had become empty streets. Maybe Koontz was right. Maybe I didn't have as firm a grip on reality as I thought.

I wasn't feeling much better when I pulled into the parking lot across from the Temple Street courthouse. Mobile units from the three major networks as well as from a couple of the local stations were positioned out front behind a police barricade that cordoned off an unruly crowd of court-house groupies, winos, and bag ladies. Despite the rain, they were all obviously waiting for Otis, and I walked quickly past them into the entrance of the civil court on Hill. The record bureau was downstairs and I hesitated only for a second before I signed my real name with the clerk. It didn't take long to look up the two names. Not surprisingly, there was no listing in California for a Bibles for Bucharest. There was no Nestral either. But there was a Nestron on Sixth Street. It was listed as a distribution company. But with no indication of what it distributed.

I hurried out of the building and headed back toward my car. But just as I turned the corner onto Hill Street, I saw the crowd surge forward. Otis, in dark glasses and a pin-striped suit, was emerging from the criminal courthouse with his manager/attorney Purvis Wilkes and three expensive-looking white lawyers with fat briefcases. They were followed by a couple of dozen reporters dangling Nikons and video cameras and chanting "Mr. King, Mr. King."

Purvis Wilkes edged Otis behind him, holding his hand up in front of the reporters while guiding his client toward a waiting limousine. "Mr. King will not be making any statements at this time."

"Mr. Wilkes, any comment on the million-dollar bail?" someone shouted.

"No comment."

"Are these gentlemen part of your defense team?"

"At this moment I am Otis's sole attorney. We're looking for someone on the California bar."

And then they came all at once: "Is it true Otis'll only be

represented by a black man?'' ''Was he high?'' ''Was it
PCP or speedballs?'' ''Are you going to plead insanity?''
''Was his father once indicted for murder?'' ''Did the movie
studio force him into psychotherapy?'' ''Did Bannister want
to be his manager?'' ''Has he always been self-destructive?''
''Has King King fled the country to avoid prosecution?''
''Do you know his whereabouts?'' ''Did Otis do this to de-
fend his brother?''

''No comment. No more questions now,'' said Wilkes, continuing to block Otis out and back him toward the limousine.

He almost had the reporters out of the way and Otis in
the limo, when the comic stopped and shouted, ''Hey, wait
a minute. See that dude?'' He pointed toward me. ''He went
all the way to New York so's I could come back here and
get my ass hung. You know the moral of that one, don't you,
all you print-freak motherfuckers?'' The reporters, seizing
their opportunity, started edging forward, cameras rolling.
''Never trust a white man, *any* white man, but *especially* one
of them civil rights–kissing, Motown-loving, Huey-hugging,
Stokely-sucking, Jesse Jackson jive-time jigaboo jelly-
hopping liberal-radical whatevers who think they gonna *save*
your ass. Just 'cause those motherfuckers was on some kinda
march twenty years ago, they think they *own* you. But they
got love and hate and guilt all so screwed up in their own
pea brains, all's they can do is *kill* you with kindness! And
with friends like that, like the dude say, who needs enemies?
So that be the Gospel According to Saint Otis. When I die
in jail, it ain't my cross they gonna nail!''

And with that he got into the limo and drove off. The
reporters and most of the crowd ran after him, trying to get

some last word. Not a bad speed rap, I thought, for someone who had been clean for at least twenty-four hours. I thought I'd better move on before the fourth estate decided to interview the object of Otis's derision, but as I started down the sidewalk, I could see the New Yorker standing there, staring at me.

18

He was still in my rearview mirror when I saw Nestron near the corner of Sixth and La Brea, a low-slung warehouse in the early sixties style with dull mustard brick walls and a shake roof. Although the light was green, I slowed as I approached La Brea, stopping at the intersection and ignoring the outraged shouts of the truckdriver behind me. Then, when the light turned red, I gunned my engine and ran it, zooming between two cars and a bus and shooting across the wet intersection onto San Vincente amidst a chorus of squeaking breaks and honking horns. I was going about seventy-five and spraying enough water to irrigate a block's worth of azaleas. Fortunately, there weren't any cops around as I made a hard right on Orange Drive and then another onto Edgewood Place. I sped through La Brea again, dodging more cars and a couple of trucks, and made my third right on Citrus Avenue. Then I pulled over to wait to see if I had lost the New Yorker. He must have been more sensible than I, because it seemed as if I had given him the slip somewhere along the line. I slid into first again and drove slowly down to the end of Citrus, entering Nestron the back way and parking beside their loading dock.

Two minutes later I was wondering what all the effort was about. The only thing Nestron distributed was stationery, and the closest it got to the pharmaceutical business was the paper for prescriptions.

I got back in my car feeling dizzy and unfocused. I knew there were things I should do, leads I should follow up, but I couldn't concentrate on them. It suddenly occurred to me it was time for my regular appointment with Nathanson, the one he had canceled. I decided to go there anyway.

The sky became darker and darker as I headed west toward Santa Monica. By the time I was descending into the canyon, it seemed like it was practically night, although, on my watch, it was only a minute past two. Had it been scheduled, I was just one minute late for my appointment. But as I approached Nathanson's house, it was clear someone had replaced me. A dark, bearded man was crossing from his car, a ten-year-old Mercedes, to the psychiatrist's office. I parked right behind him and jumped out. As if driven by unconscious forces, I rushed past him and into the door.

Nathanson looked up, startled, from his desk as I entered.

"What, Moses?"

"I know this isn't my appointment."

"Yes, you didn't reschedule."

"I want to know why you canceled it."

"Another client had an emergency."

He turned toward the door where the dark, bearded man

was standing with a baffled expression. "It's all right," the man said in an extremely deferential voice. "I'll go."

"No," said Nathanson, "that won't be necessary."

"I also have to know what you were doing in Koreatown."

Nathanson hesitated. "Give us a couple of minutes," he said to his other patient.

"Yes, of course, Doctor." He exited, shutting the door carefully behind him.

"Sit down, Moses."

"No, I'll stand." I glanced over at his desk. The matches had vanished from atop the book from the Board of Medical Examiners.

"Your eyes are crystallized. The woman. How are things with the woman?"

"Bad."

"I thought so. Tell me about it."

"What? Tell *me* about what *you* were doing down there with that reverend."

"Center yourself in the here and now. What is going on with you at this very moment?"

"Don't give me that psychobabble! What the fuck is going on?" I stood over him, looking down at his chair as if I were ready to shake it.

"I can't tell you. And if I could, I wouldn't."

"Why not?"

"Because I'm the wrong place to hear it."

"What?"

"You have to figure this out for yourself. No more gurus, Moses."

"I don't want a guru. I want the truth!"

"If you want the truth, you're going to have to see what's around you. Start focusing on the present. Concentrate on your breathing."

"Is that *all* you have to say to me?"

"At the moment, yes."

I stared at him for a second. "I'm finished with therapy and do you know what else? I'm going to see you get arrested!"

"Good. *Now* you're taking control."

I walked out, slamming the door in his face. I continued right past the other patient in the used Mercedes and into my car, turning on the motor and roaring out of there. I was halfway to Koreatown before I knew where I was going. But when I did, the cobwebs were gone from my brain. All my senses were heightened and my body was alert. It was as if I had just spent a year in the dark and I was finally coming out into the daylight.

I pulled up across from the New Inchon and went in. It was the middle of the afternoon, the dead hour for restaurants, but there were still some men at the bar knocking down the well drinks. I slipped in next to two of them and ordered a shot of Glenlivet.

"You know, it's not just the labor costs," I said to them before the bartender even came back with my drink. The two men looked at each other, naturally confused about what this gringo was saying. "I mean the quality's not bad. But nobody's going to tell me that Gold Star and Samsung are better than Sony and Hitachi, at least not yet. So there's got to be some reason Korea's the next wave, the next industrial power. And you know what it is? Faith. Plain old-fashioned faith." The bartender poured out my scotch and passed it in my direction. "Thanks, Joe. . . . You know what I mean?" I said to the guys.

"Yes, yes. Sort of." The one nearest me, a bulbous fellow in a red tie, smiled in embarrassment.

"What it is," I continued, "is that Korea combines Oriental patience with Christian steadfastness. Now, you tell me one other culture with that combination."

They looked at each other as if to say where did this guy get off the boat. Only *they* were the ones off the boat and I was the hometown boy.

"Not all Koreans are Christians," said the bulbous one. "Some are Buddhist, some are Confucian."

"Same difference. Look, tell you what I mean. Who are your biggest evangelists in Koreatown today? You know, the top dogs."

"Dr. Chung," said bulbous.

"Dr. Wu," chimed in his buddy.

"Chung? He's the one with the Mercedes stretch limo, isn't he?"

"No, that's Wu," said bulbous.

"Yeah, right. He's the one with that church over on . . ."

"Dr. Wu's church is not here. It is in Seoul."

"Yes, but he has the office building on Eighth and Crenshaw," said the buddy.

"That's just my point. A businessman. He knows the Lord wants us all to prosper. Right? Your health." I downed my scotch and exited.

Five minutes later I was in front of the Hankyu Investment Center on Eighth and Crenshaw. I walked past a realty, a brokerage firm, and a coffee shop called The 38th Parallel into the lobby and found the building index by the elevator. There was no listing for a Dr. Wu or a Reverend Wu or indeed for a religious organization of any sort. But my eye did stop on one particular name: the VIP Leasing Corporation. It was the same Bahamian outfit that owned Carl Bannister's tony Malibu property and it happened to be the penthouse suite.

I got into the elevator by myself and pressed "P." It was eleven floors up and I was going along pretty well until we got to five and the elevator stopped. The doors opened and the Chu's Brothers got in.

"Hey, smart dog," said the verbal Chu. "How are you this afternoon?" He took out a .38 and pointed it at me.

"Getting worse by the moment."

"We gonna change directions. See what's happening in the basement."

"Yeah, I hear that's where they embalmed Sid Vicious."

"You like punk music, smart dog. Good." He pressed the emergency button, stopping the elevator.

"Particularly religious punk music. It's inspirational."

"Yeah. In tongues." He said the last word long and hard as his brother grabbed my neck in a choker and pulled me back against the wall. The verbal Chu laughed softly and pressed "B." We were going down.

The basement was a series of corridors leading toward a boiler room. The Chu's pushed me all the way in the back to a laundry and shoved me inside, shutting the door behind us.

"Well, Brother Chu, we gonna kill him here and carry him out? Or carry him out and then kill him?"

"Kill me here," I said. "Then dump me in Joshua Tree National Monument. That's a great place. In the sixties they burned somebody alive there. In a hearse."

"Flaming hearse . . . wow," said the verbal Chu.

"Of course, there are other possibilities. There's the cactus under the Hollywood sign. An actress committed suicide that way, stripped naked. And then the PCH. Back in the thirties, a German director named Murnau went flying off a cliff there in his car while his boyfriend was sucking his cock."

"I like that," said the silent Chu, opening his mouth for the first time.

"And wait a minute. . . . How about the bushes in Elysian Park? That's where Angelo Buono—you know, the Hillside Strangler—used to drag women to rape and kill them. And what about the immortal Richard Ramirez, the Night Stalker?"

"Yeah, heavy metal Satanism!" said the verbal Chu.

"Whips and chains. Can you dig it? There are so many possibilities in this world. Like you could garrote a guy with a spike or . . . check this." I picked up one of the towels from the top of the washer. "Even a common household item can be great for torture. The Chinese used water, right? And the Shah of Iran, I hear his boys used to wrap ordinary electric wire around the balls of his prisoners and give 'em a jolt. Let 'em know who was *really* boss. Great, huh? How about this?" I dangled the towel at arm's length by my side.

"The white flag. They say a bull will only charge at red but ... what about a bully?" I jiggled the towel again. The verbal Chu looked over at it and I rushed him, sending him sprawling and the gun flying behind the dryer. I dove on him, pushing off his sunglasses and sticking my fingers in his eyes the way I had been taught in my Tae Kwan Do course. Then I rolled over and kicked his brother in the face with the back of my heel. It was all about fighting dirty. Before they knew what had happened, I was crawling across the floor and grabbing the gun barrel, which was sticking out from under the bottom of the machine. I jumped to my feet, training it on them, feeling my hand shaking and face flushed with blood. I hated violence. It always made me want to throw up.

"All right, fuckheads, who're you working for?"

Both Chu's stared at me dazedly, blood dripping from the nose and mouth of one and from the eyes of the other.

"C'mon, guys, you don't want to suck lead from this baby." I held the .38 closer for their edification. The Chu's still did not react. I kicked the nearest one, the silent partner, in the face again, catching him right across the cheekbone. His head snapped back and I heard a crack.

"Reverend Wu," he said. "We're workin' for Reverend Wu."

"That's more like it. What did he want you to do?"

More silence.

"What is this? The last rerun of *I've Got a Secret?*" I started to raise my foot again.

"We don't know. We don't know," the silent partner

gasped. The verbal Chu had been reduced to nothing but unintelligible moans, rolling on his back and clutching his eyes in pain like a punk Oedipus. "We never met him."

"You never *met* the guy you're working for?"

"We take orders from his helpers."

"What orders?"

"Anything they want. They give us a clothing allowance. You know, for Melrose."

"Clothes," I said. "Jesus." I stared down at them. Two Korean punks beaten to a pulp. For the first time, I was seeing the Chu's in clear light without their dark glasses, even if it was only the green fluorescents of the laundry room. At the most, they were fifteen, maybe sixteen years old—depressing, vicious little creeps, like bit players in a Twisted Sister video.

"Don't turn us in, mister, please," said the silent brother. "My uncle'll kill us. . . . Right, Douglas?"

He looked over at his brother, but Douglas was too sick to respond. He spat a tooth out on the floor.

I shoved the gun under my jacket and left. It wasn't until I was riding up the elevator again that I noticed the sleeve was spattered with blood. My best jacket, I thought. Christ. And then I smiled as I rubbed the blood in so it blended with the multicolored weave of the Italian wool. I was just like the rest of them: another clothes horse.

I adjusted my tie and stepped out at the penthouse, emerging in the foyer of VIP Leasing. It was the kind of all-purpose office reception area that could have been anywhere in America and, by now, anywhere in the world—avocado green shag carpet, ersatz walnut paneling, and mock Renaissance brass table lamps. The receptionist was hunched over a high-tech telephone installation, pushing buttons and trying to look busy.

"Hello, I'm Phil Bettelheim. I'd like to see Dr. Wu if you don't mind." I took out one of my handy-dandy little business cards and handed it to her.

"Does he know you?"

"I don't believe he does. I'm with the INS—the Immigration and Naturalization Service." I said it slowly so she got it. "One of your employees, a"—I pretended to glance at a scrawled address—"Douglas Chu of Laveta Terrace, has recently become a winner in the new California Lottery."

"He has?" Her eyes widened.

"Fortunately or unfortunately. You see, a couple of weeks ago, when a certain Jorge Esperanza won the grand prize, the Roswell Baking Company of Torrance was considerably inconvenienced when it was determined that Esperanza was an illegal alien, resulting in an investigation of their company that sent roughly eighty percent of their employees back to Mexico and Guatemala. Now, I'm sure—"

I would've continued, but by now the receptionist was on the phone, jabbering away urgently in rapid-fire Korean. In somewhere around thirty seconds, Dr. Wu's personal secretary, a carefully coiffed woman in a silky Hong Kong–style slit skirt and long vermilion fingernails, arrived in the foyer to escort me to his office. Not that I could've gotten lost. The heavy bronze doors with the marble handles at the end of the corridor were a dead giveaway.

Wu himself was about five feet tall and sat behind a desk about twice as wide. He reminded me of pictures I had seen of Deng Xiaoping at state receptions, his feet dangling about six inches above the floor. He wasn't as smart as Deng, but he wasn't bad, and the minute he saw me, he signaled for his secretary to get out, as well as one of his "helpers," a snakelike individual wearing a white turtleneck and an ankh who had been leaning against the bookshelf trying not to pick his teeth.

"Sit down," he said, not taking his eyes off me. I sank into a soft leather armchair that lowered me down to near his level. "You're not the INS. You don't look like them, you don't dress like them, and your eyes are too intelligent. What do you want?"

"I want to know why you killed Mike Ptak."

He didn't flinch a centimeter. "You're the second person to ask me that this week. I don't kill people. I'm far too rich for that."

"That sounds good, Doctor. But it doesn't jibe with my experience and I'm sure it doesn't jibe with yours. When it's not a member of their own family, people usually kill to advance or protect a position. My assumption is you killed Ptak—or more likely had him killed—to protect a position."

"What was that?"

I took a flyer. "About twenty-five million in aid funds."

"That's a lot of money."

"Yes, it is."

"And then you had to get rid of a Romanian bellhop named Vasile Nastase, who, because of his religious devotion, you were able to manipulate to your own ends."

"Because of his devotion?" He shook his head. "What is your name? You are a private investigator, no doubt." I told him. "Well, Mr. Wine, let me explain some of the simple facts of life to you. When you are doing God's work, you have nothing to fear from a Mr. Ptak or from anybody else. The New Evangelical Church of the Eastern Gate is an entirely nonprofit religious organization headquartered in Seoul, Korea. According to the laws of that country and of this one—the separation of church and state admired by every schoolchild—no one is entitled to examine our books or to inspect our accounts unless they can show evidence of a felony, like mail fraud. That can take years. Indeed, it usually does." He half smiled.

"And VIP Leasing?"

"A small real estate holding company. A church is entitled to hold real estate, is it not? Compared to the Vatican, we are but a dot in the universe."

"I find it interesting that the real estate you're holding was the Malibu residence of a Dr. Carl Bannister, whose recent murder was connected to the other two deaths."

"Interesting, yes. But hardly conclusive. And I understand there has been an arrest in that regard. Now, Mr. Wine, you must excuse me. If you think I had something directly to do with these deaths, you must prove it for yourself. But I assure you, you are wasting your time." He stood up and bowed to me. "And if you do insist on carrying on these investigations, it will be at your peril. Not because of these alleged crimes, but because *every* organization has things to hide. It is the nature of human society. Your culture is filled with corruption. So is mine. So is the Russian and so, no doubt, are the Chinese, the Italian, and the Greek. You may think it is good to root it out, but many lives depend upon

these structures, whole systems. The person who tries to pu-
rify the world must bear the consequences of his idealism.''

"I appreciate your analysis of history, but, uh, one thing
is troubling me, Doctor: the IRS. Don't they figure into this
somehow? I seem to recall the Reverend Moon had some
problems with them.''

"That fool.'' Wu frowned. "My daughter married at that
absurd mass wedding of his.''

I grinned. "You mean that publicity stunt when he married a thousand Moonies simultaneously?'' I glanced at the
framed portrait of a young Korean girl on the bookshelf
behind him. It was about a ten-year-old picture and the girl
seemed around fourteen, but she was oddly familiar.

"Exhibitionists like that deserve whatever fate they get,''
Wu continued. "But as for the IRS, they are no problem.
You simply list your expenses and your program services on
their Form Nine-ninety.''

"Program services?''

"Education, promotion, and aid.''

"All mixed in one?''

"Peculiar, isn't it? But in any case, Mr. Wine, it's irrelevant. For the greedy there are many better ways to hide
money.''

"You mean like cash in the mail? I hear you get tons of
that, particularly after a natural disaster like the Mexican
earthquake. And I imagine those small checks aren't hard
to convert, either. I mean it'd be hell to cross-check, wouldn't
it? Lying on our income tax about charitable donations is
practically a national sport.''

The Reverend half smiled again. Maybe this is what they meant about the Mysterious East. It wasn't all that mysterious.

"So what do you do with all that cash? It's kind of tricky, walking into a bank with a suitcase of, say, ten million and offering it all at once to the lady in new accounts."

The smile disappeared from his face.

"I suppose you'd have to do what any self-respecting drug dealer does," I went on. "Open a business and slowly filter the money in. But you couldn't do that all at once. You'd need someplace to keep the cash while you were waiting to put it there."

"I imagine you would, Mr. Wine."

"I wonder where that would be."

"Why don't you have a look?" He opened the door for me. "I don't think the Chu's Brothers will disturb you. Good to have met you, Mr. Wine. God bless."

I exited the building and got into my car, driving off a few blocks and then slowly back along Ninth. I parked in a 7-Eleven and walked back toward the Hankyu Investment Center through a long driveway that ran behind the shops that fronted Crenshaw. I had noticed on the way out that the entire building was wired with closed-circuit television and, Chu's or no Chu's, I wasn't sure I wanted to go back in. So I stopped in the rear parking area and looked into the detective's friend, the garbage dumpster. It wasn't my favorite kind of work. But I had long since given up whatever squeamishness I had at this method of investigation, because nobody, not even Bob Dylan or the CIA, shredded *all* their papers. Something always slipped through, even if it was just a phone number scribbled on a check from the local Mexican take-out.

Fortunately, this particular dumpster wasn't loaded with yesterday's guacamole, or even kim chee. It was stacked to the gills with printouts, readouts, and all the rest of the detritus of our microprint age. Within about five minutes I could quote the Dow Jones averages for the last week, cite the Standard & Poor's ratings on at least five up-and-coming corporations, and knew the prices of gold, silver, platinum, and Krugerrands. Koontz was right: the whole world was going berserk on integrated business software.

I was about to give up and go to real estate school, when I pulled out yet another printout from under a pile of insurance brochures. It was titled: CURRENT AFFILI-ATES—NEW EVANGELICAL CHURCH OF THE EASTERN GATE. I skimmed down the alphabetical list but stopped right off on the second entry: BIBLES FOR BUCHAREST—CON-TACT: W. T. WEBSTER, 46 AVONDALE, GLENDALE. I glanced up at the penthouse. The sun was beginning to set, turn-ing the office window of Reverend Wu a smoky orange. I stuffed the list in my pocket and headed back for my car.

Thirty minutes later I was cruising slowly up Avondale. It was one of those ramshackle neighborhoods in the flats of Glendale that probably hadn't changed much since the first Okies and Arkies came out to California during the days of the Dust Bowl. This was Bible country, the kind of place they still pronounced "roof" as "ruff" and Sting was some-thing you got from a bee.

Number 46 was the second to last house on the block, a decrepit affair in the bungalow style with eaves that were painted a nasty yellow and faded green asbestos siding. Some golden bamboo had run wild near the front porch and I could see it protruding through the concrete steps as I climbed up to the front door. There wasn't a bell, so I pulled back the torn screen and knocked firmly on the inner jamb. I could hear the Five Blind Boys of Alabama singing "Carry Me Up" on a scratchy record somewhere inside and I half expected the faces to be black, but it was a young white man in his early twenties who opened the door, keeping it on a chain that was long enough to see about a third of his face, which was blotched with psoriasis. He wore a set of braces on upper teeth that looked heavily corroded by sugar.

"You ain't sellin' and I ain't buyin'," he said before I could open my mouth.

"I'm not a salesman."

"So?"

"Tell 'im to go away," came the voice of an old woman from within.

"He ain't comin' in, Granma." He brought his eye closer to the door and peered at me. "Whaddaya want?" I recognized his voice from someplace, but I wasn't sure where. Then I remembered. The phone call.

"I'm a Christian," I said.

"The devil you are!" He turned away. "We got a liar out here, Granma!"

"We better call the police. I'm gonna call 'em right now, Billy."

"Where are the medicines, Billy?" I said.

"What is this? You get away from here. You ain't supposed to come here. . . . Granma, you got the police?"

"Uh-huh. I'm talkin' to 'em now. You want the small-bore or the recoilless?"

Billy didn't say anything.

"What happened to Stanley Burckhardt?"

"Who?"

"Fat man, around fifty. A private dick."

"That wasn't my business. They took him away."

"Who? The Koreans?"

"Ain't no Koreans in this. Koreans religious people, holy people."

I grabbed Billy by the shirt and pulled him to the door. *"Who took Burckhardt?"*

"I was tryin' to help you, mister, and now you tryin' to get me killed. You ain't supposed to be here. Get away. Get away. . . . Granma, get that small-bore. Granma, fast!"

"You're the guy who put Burckhardt on my tail, aren't you? The twenty-three-year-old."

"Someone was lyin' to us. They said they was holy people. They said they was with the Korean, but they wasn't."

"You mean whoever convinced Vasile to let them into the penthouse of the Picasso pretended they were part of the Reverend Wu's church?"

Billy nodded frantically. "They knew all about it. They promised us Bibles."

"But you guys didn't know they were gonna get rid of Ptak, did you? Commit a cardinal sin. And now you're feeling guilty."

"You gonna get me killed. I know'd it. Just like poor Vasile. I swore I'd never tell. I swore. Lord have mercy on those who do His work. Granma!"

"Unburden yourself, Billy. Repent! Who was it?"

Through the window slat, I could see the shadow of the old woman outlined against a church calendar as she advanced toward the door with a shotgun.

"A dark-haired guy. Thin face." I described the New Yorker for him.

"I ain't gonna tell you, mister. I ain't ever gonna tell you." He suddenly slid down against the door, slumping to his knees and leaving me staring straight at Granma who was pointing the small-bore in my face with a lunatic gleam in her eyes.

"Turn tail, boy!" She cocked the gun for emphasis, but she didn't need to. I already had the distinct impression she meant it.

"It's okay. It's okay," I said, backing away past an old rusted-out Dodge parked in their driveway.

I got in my car and drove down the block, parking around the corner of the next intersection. In about five minutes a couple of prowl cars roared up the street, their sirens wailing. I sat there for a while, thumbing through Sandollar's *Billboard,* waiting for them to leave and wondering who, if it wasn't the Koreans, had Billy so frightened. It was clear that whoever it was had duped Nastase into allowing him or them into the penthouse, drugged Ptak, bumped him off, and then took care of Nastase and probably Burckhardt to keep it covered up. No wonder Billy was panicked. With a record like that, who wouldn't be? It was a lot more than he bargained for when he signed up to enlighten godless commies with Bibles for Bucharest.

In about ten minutes, one of the cop cars came by with Billy and his grandmother ensconced in the backseat. I figured the other one was waiting back at their house for my return. But by then I wasn't that interested. My attention was elsewhere. It was focused on the full-page ad on the back of *Billboard*.

19 Two hours later I was still staring at the ad, pacing about my apartment and trying to put the pieces together, when the bell rang. I opened the door and Chantal burst in, wearing a cloche hat and a black trench coat. She started talking the moment she entered. "Look, I know apologies are useless, but I'm sorry. It was stupid of me, getting up and blabbing in front of all those people. I never should've done it. I was just too headstrong to admit it. You get that way, don't you? Take a position and you can't back off and then you regret it ten minutes later?"

"If it's ten minutes later, I usually try to come back and patch things up as quickly as possible."

"Well, that's not me. I mean, not usually. I *never* go back.

But I'm here now. Doesn't that count for something?'' She looked at me hopefully. ''Anyway, whatever happens, I couldn't drop the case just like that. I mean, it's pretty interesting and everything. So this morning I decided to follow Emily again, and I took some pictures you might want to look at.'' She put a manila envelope on my coffee table.

''Pictures, huh?'' I looked at her. She had turned around and was facing the sofa, tapping her toe and staring at the ceiling, trying not to look nervous. This woman was something—the most extreme case of tough/tender I had encountered since Barbara Stanwyck in *Golden Boy*. I had to admit it—I was thrilled she was back.

''Aren't you going to take your coat off?'' I said.

''Oh, yeah. Sure.'' She wheeled around, peeling off the hat first. Her red hair cascaded down on the black coat.

''Look, uh,'' I continued, trying to stick to business, ''you know that gorgeous Art Deco wreck on Sunset, the building right down the hill here?''

''You mean Astro House? The one everyone dreams about remodeling?''

''Yeah. But no one thinks it's really worth the investment.'' I walked up to her and put the *Billboard* in her hand, pointing to the back page. ''Look.''

She stared down at a slick airbrushed layout of a 1930s-type Chrysler Building skyscraper dominating the Strip. Little miniature DC-3's were circling its spire as they did in the old Universal Pictures logo with RKO-like radio waves shooting out of its antenna in the form of musical notes. Down below a line of Maseratis, Porsches, and Lamborghinis awaited a parking valet beneath a large porte cochere with the name of the establishment written in brilliant rose neon across the top: Neutron City.

"Neutron City . . ." she repeated.

"Sounds familiar, doesn't it?"

She looked at me, puzzled.

"Could that have been what Mike was shouting from the penthouse? Not nestron, neutral, or nastral. Or even neuter. But Neutron . . ." I took the magazine from her and read from the ad copy: " 'Future Home of the World's Greatest Recording Studio and Radio Broadcast Facility. The New Capitol of Pop at the Old Astro Building. The Past Lives in the Future and the Future Lives in the Past in this *Multi-million-dollar* State-of-the-Art Renovation that Begins Next Week. Who Says that Rock 'n' Roll Is Dead? Reserve Space at the Neutron Now. Contact: 555-3023.' "

"What's that?"

"According to the Haines Directory"—I gestured to my microfiche, which had a reverse phone book on film—"it's something called Sassafras Productions."

"Who're they?"

"Well, I don't know for sure, but I just spent an hour at Tower Records, snooping around the oldies bin, and it's a pretty strange coincidence. Remember that group about five years ago, the Headless Chickens?"

"The one with the creepy bass player in the clear vinyl jump suit?"

"Right. The guy who bit live animals on stage for p.r.? Anyway, that was a Sassafras Production for Licorice Records."

"Sandollar's old company." She looked back down at the *Billboard* ad. "A multi-million-dollar renovation," she said. "I thought he was sick of the music business."

"It's an addiction. He told me himself."

"*And* he's supposed to be broke."

"Yeah. Funny, isn't it? You'd think with his track record, no one would touch him."

"Then where'd he get the . . . ?" She stopped and looked at me.

I didn't answer.

"Cosmic Aid." She let the words out slowly.

I nodded.

"Out of the mouths of starving Africans . . ."

"Into the ears of the people who wanted to feed them. Nice trick, huh?"

"What a prick," she said. "What an incredible prick."

"Yeah, twenty-five millions' worth. And I bet he doesn't leave tracks. He's probably keeping it all in cash and we'd have to show where he got it in the first place. With a charity, that could take years."

"Well," she said. "Now I'm really sure you ought to look at those pictures."

20

"So you don't like her pictures," I said. "That's kind of an insult, you know. The lady was a professional photographer in D.C. for two years."

"I didn't say I didn't like her pictures. I just said the risk entailed is more than the possible gain."

"More than the gain? Right now you've got one client hiding under a rock and the other one's being railroaded onto Death Row."

"I wouldn't worry about that. California hasn't pulled the plug on anybody since Caryl Chessman."

"Yeah, but they've kept a lot of people waiting."

It was the following night and I was riding through South L.A. in the back of a rented T-Bird. Chantal was sitting next to me. Purvis Wilkes, Otis's manager/lawyer, was in the front next to a black behemoth named Omar, who as yet hadn't said one word.

"Look, I want to see the man himself," I said. "I'm sure he's capable of making his own decisions."

"He's not in L.A."

"Don't give me that shit, Purvis. His brother's up against the wall and if he wasn't here, we wouldn't be this far along in the first place."

At that point, we were making a right onto Slauson, not

more than a few blocks from where, about a dozen years ago, the SWAT team dusted the SLA in their safe house. We made another right onto Compton and continued through the invisible county line where, for reasons known only to some long-deceased bureaucrat, the city of L.A. became the city of Florence and then became L.A. again in the section the world knew as Watts, famed for its riot and for its subsequent generations of Eastern tourists who would gawk and say, "It doesn't look *so* bad here."

But the four of us in the car weren't saying anything as we drove, continuing past the Rodia Towers and the old Red Car tracks until we turned once more onto a tiny side street lined with rusted oil barrels and junked cars called 111th Place. A couple of brothers in black berets and motorcycle jackets with skull and bones on the back were standing at the front end by one of the cars when we rounded the corner. We slowed as we approached them, waiting for them to nod before we moved on. I glanced over at Chantal who was staring calmly in front of her with her fingers tucked under my leg. Two houses ahead, I saw a light go on in the window and then go off.

We veered behind a row of barrels, bouncing over a lawn, and pulled up along the side of that house. Chantal and I started out of the car, when two other brothers emerged as if out of nowhere, thrust us up against the hood of the T-Bird, and began to pat us down. Wilkes watched, half smiling. When they were satisfied we were clean, they led us into the house. Wilkes followed a few steps behind while Omar, never moving from the car, sat and waited.

The living room was totally dark when we got in. In the

filtered window light, I could just make out the figure of
King King sitting in the corner smoking a thin cigar. He
waited for us to sit on the couch before he spoke.

"You cause problems, cowboy. Problems in the entertainment business and problems in . . . the pleasure business."

"I think they'd have problems of their own."

"And you brought a bitch. You didn't say you were bringing a bitch."

"She's my partner."

"I don't trust men who work with bitches. They get led
around by their cock."

"What about women who work with men?" said Chantal.
"What do they get led around by?"

"I haven't figured that one out yet." King King laughed
softly and smoked awhile. "So you have some pictures."

"You interested?"

"I don't know. This thing is a great risk."

"Yes, it is. It seems they're very well protected. Even
better than I thought."

"And this has to be done now?"

"So I'm informed."

"How many do you provide?"

"Just the two of us."

"And the rest are supposed to come from me."

"Four good people would be enough. Any more and it
could be cumbersome. That's c-u-m—" The look on his face
said he wasn't in the mood to make an addition to his private
dictionary.

"And what happens to the money?"

"It can't go back into your business."

"You are a moralist, Mr. Wine."

"No, I just don't think much of what you do."

"I don't think much of what you do, either. And I still say you are a moralist."

"As you wish."

"And what about my brother? Will this free my brother?"

"There are no guarantees."

King King shrugged and shook his head.

"Perhaps you should see the pictures," said Chantal.

He shrugged again. "As you wish."

Chantal reached into her purse as one of the brothers who escorted us in took out a pocket flashlight and handed it to King. Suddenly someone started to come in through the kitchen door.

"Get out of here!" King shouted.

"Hey, what the fuck? I do what I want. I the one who's out on bail here. You the fugitive from justice." It was Otis.

"I'm the fugitive and you're the moron. I told you a hundred times, every minute you're seen with me is another year down the road to self-destruction."

"I jus' wanna have a look at this white boy here." He walked over to me and stared in my eyes. "Hi, white boy. I got you a little publicity on the six o'clock news the other day, didn't I? Sorry about that. You know us crazy black motherfuckahs. We schizomatic. One day we hates ya, one day we loves ya. It's just like you Jewish motherfuckers— two thousand years of rocky road makes you walk funny even when it's flat. And I wanna tell you one other thing: if you save my ass, I'm gonna hate you for it. I know that sounds weird, but that's the way life is and we all gotta live with it."

I took the photographs from Chantal and walked over to King, who flicked on the flashlight, training it on the picture on the top of the pile. It showed three tiered concrete-block buildings notched into the end of a valley surrounded with eucalyptus and live oak. "That's the headquarters of Cosmic Aid."

"Looks like a cross between a minimum security prison and a bomb shelter. Where is it?"

"Up a hidden dirt road several miles outside of Ojai, California."

"Hey, I been there," said Otis. "Shangri-La. Where they filmed *Lost Horizon*. Camera dude took me up there one time to score some mushrooms."

"Not this time," said King.

Otis stared at his brother. "I ain't goin' with you, sonofabitch. Think I'd go with you?"

"Damn right you're not. You're staying right where those movie people want you in that fancy hotel in Beverly Hills. And you're gonna wear a tie and walk around the lobby, talking white with Purvis and looking like the nicest black boy that ever came out of the Bronx. . . . Reggie. Hey, Reggie." One of the bodyguards appeared out of the shadows. "Make sure Otis gets home."

"Yassa, boss. Yassa, massa!" said Otis. He did a shuffle, still staring back at his brother as he followed Reggie out.

I flipped to the next photo. "That's the security gate.

Three-quarters of a mile of chain link fence that rings the property. You'll note the barbed wire at the top and the high-voltage connectors."

"Noted."

I went on to the next one, a closer angle of the compound itself, several eager young people walking purposefully between the buildings as if they were on a crucial mission. "Those are some of the workers, all very idealistic, all believing they're helping to save the world. Several we talked to came down from the Rajneeshpuram after the Oregon courts closed it down." The following photo was a night shot of five men in paramilitary outfits running across a field behind the headquarters building. Each one carried what looked like a 308-caliber Steyr gun. "Their security force," I said. "They don't come outside in the daytime."

"How'd you get that?"

"Ask her." I nodded to Chantal.

"A Sun Pac Twenty-two flash with an infrared head," she said. "Works on any camera if you're inside fifty feet."

I flipped to a closer shot of one of them, my friend the New Yorker, crouched in the darkness instructing the others in hand-to-hand combat. "This is their leader. Considering the burn scars on his back, my guess is he was Special Forces in Vietnam or Laos. Maybe someplace else, but whatever it is, he knows his business." I continued to the next photograph: a long-lens shot of a black Saab Turbo with opaque windows. A man and two women were getting out, crossing to a side entrance.

"Sandollar!" said King.

I nodded.

"And look at that—Mike Ptak's bitch. Who's the other one?"

"His wife, Kim. A Korean."

"What're they into? Trios?"

"No. I just think they're into money."

"Fuckin' Ptak."

"Fuckin' Ptak wanted to stop it. It's his wife that didn't want to. That's my guess, anyway. He's the one who got tossed off the Picasso. Not her."

"Anyone else in on it with them?"

I hesitated. "I'm not sure at the moment. I hope not."

"What do you mean you hope not?"

"Look, are you in on this or not? Your brother's being hung out to dry for some white asshole's rock 'n' roll dream, and millions of dollars are being stolen out of the mouths of African babies."

"Where do they keep this money?"

"We don't know," said Chantal. "I went in yesterday afternoon, pretending to be a volunteer. You don't get much farther than the front desk."

"But you're sure it's there?"

"Nothing's sure," I said. "But I don't know what all the security's about if it's not."

21 "Fifty thousand if you prove him innocent?"

"I wouldn't do this for nothing."

"It's not enough. You should've gotten more for that. But anyway, I'm glad to hear it. I was beginning to think you were a fucking liberal idiot."

"Not me, King. I'm a monarchist."

"What?"

"M-o-n—"

"Don't condescend to me, boy. I don't bring my notebook into situations like this."

It was the next night and we were headed north on Highway 63 in a rented Ford Bronco—Chantal, King, Omar, and I, plus two more of King's entourage: one, a fat mulatto with a clublike right arm, who was known as Lancaster; the other, a dapper, handsome man in a cableknit sweater with a faint African accent and a briar pipe who was called Drill. We were all armed but only with the intention of self-defense. This was to be surgery—quick, deft, and out—not a protective reaction strike.

The road wound up into the mountains, past the little blue-flower signs that denoted a scenic road and the offers of VIEW LOTS—FOR SALE BY OWNER and the truck farms and the isolated stretches of housing tracts that seemed to pop out of nowhere, banding together like pioneers against Indians who had been gone for centuries. The night was overcast and Omar switched on the windshield wipers to stop us from misting over. The road itself was still damp, the weather of the last day never having really left, but come and gone in short fronts.

We hit the intersection for 150 and I told Omar not to turn for Ojai, but to drive straight toward Meiners Oaks. After another couple of miles, we reached a stone bridge where a dry riverbed slipped under the highway and became a rock basin. Just beyond was the dirt road that cut through the notch toward Cosmic Aid.

We took it and bounced along the potholes for a few hundred yards before the road started to go up at a steep grade, closing in about every fifty feet with large ceanothus branches brushing against the windshield. A pair of coyotes ran along in front of us and disappeared down a ravine. We rounded a corner, skidding toward the edge of a sharp curve, our headlights beaming out in the darkness, and then slid to our right, coming out on the other side overlooking the canyon. The Cosmic Aid Foundation was visible below us, the few building lights that were still on dwarfed by the large arcs that illuminated the complex.

"Turn 'em off," I said, and Omar extinguished our headlights.

We began our descent, moving slowly back and forth along the switchbacks, inching forward on the narrow road until we had rounded another corner and were out of sight of the Foundation again. Once more Omar put on the high beams.

"Sonofabitch," said King. "We're city boys." It had

started to rain again, pelting down on the windshield in large glops somewhere between hail and sleet. "We don't have no business out here at two in the morning."

"Would you rather be at an after-hours club?"

There were murmurs of approval from King's pals.

"Over there," said Chantal, pointing out a fork where an even narrower road fell off to the left with the suddenness of a ski run.

"We better get what we came for, Wine."

The Bronco jounced down the smaller road until the brush got so thick we couldn't go any further without a tractor in front of us.

"We thought we'd camp here," said Chantal. "The fence is only about a hundred yards off down that trail."

The rain was starting to come down really heavy now as Omar backed up a few feet and set the emergency brake.

"What're we supposed to do? Sleep in the mud?" said King.

"We'll have to try to sleep in the car," I said. "Then go out just before dawn, as planned."

"We won't be able to see anything in this weather."

"And if we try to go out now, we'd be lucky to make it to the fork. This whole road probably washes out in about an hour."

"Great for getting aid to Ethiopia."

We slept about three hours in the Bronco, or tried to, Chantal with her head against my shoulder and me with my knee wedged under the steering column and my feet tucked under the gas pedal just beneath the heel of Omar's size thirteen boot. King was in the back with Lancaster and Drill, their broad shoulders pressed together, desperately trying for some rest like overnight passengers in the crowded waiting room of some awful Third World train station.

By three-thirty I gave up and opened my eyes. The rain had tapered off to a dull drizzle. When I turned around, I saw King staring at me, wide awake. I wondered if he could sleep in the country. For many years *I* couldn't. And he was a businessman, not used to this sort of field work, although I was sure many years ago he had to prove himself with his fists and no doubt with blades as well in the old neighborhood before achieving his vaunted executive status. Drill too was awake, humming some strange indecipherable melody to himself, when the beam of a high-powered flashlight danced through the interior of the car.

"You all right in there?" came a voice from behind us. We turned to see a man in his thirties in a Gore-Tex parka and a cowboy hat approaching with a woman about the same age in heavy rain gear right out of the Eddie Bauer catalog. They tramped down toward us, coming up along the right side of the Bronco.

"Are you stuck?" said the woman.

"It's okay," I said. "We just took a wrong turn and then the rains came."

"Yeah, we had a lot of problems ourselves," said the man. "But we're almost home—the Cosmic Aid headquarters. It's less than a mile up the road. We'll send the tow truck for you."

"That won't be necessary," I said.

"You sure?" The man looked inside our car, puzzled,

staring right at the burlap sacks where our weapons were stowed. "Funny a vehicle like this would get stuck."

"It's not stuck. We're just resting."

"We are on ze way from San Diego to San Francisco," said Chantal in a thick French accent. "On ze scenic highway when we got lost. We had to stop and do a relax."

"Tourists, huh?" said the man, who was wearing a button that said REMEMBER THE BHAGWAN. "Well, it's a beautiful route. Don't miss Big Sur. And the Seventeen-Mile Drive. And eat at Nepenthe's. Henry Miller used to hang out there."

"Ah, Henri Meel-air. Zank you. Zank you," said Chantal, laying it on thick.

"*Je vous en prie,*" said the man in horrible French. "And holler if you've got any problems." He started off with the woman, who was still looking back at us with a puzzled expression. "Our foundation would be glad to do anything we can. We're a helping institution." They disappeared into the darkness.

"Fuck," said King, glancing over at Drill, who didn't say a word.

None of us could sleep for the next hour.

By five-twenty the first gray hint of predawn light was permeating the valley. We got out of the car and buckled on our weapons, steadying ourselves in the mud and heading down the trail through a morning ground fog so thick it made the night seem clear. The sound of barking coyotes mixed with the intermittent buzz of the fencewire generator as we marched, Chantal and I up front and Omar in the rear with an Uzi. We reached the fence quickly and the rest of us lay back while Drill attached a volt-ohm meter to three points along the post. Then he isolated a piece of cable and, with extraordinary dexterity, sliced through two layers of plastic sheath with a buck knife and separated the neutral wire from the hot wire. There was a brief spark along the fence top and then everything went dead. Omar and Lancaster jumped forward with crimpers and Drill showed them exactly where he wanted the links cut.

In five minutes we were through the fence and running along the perimeter through the courtyard and around the side of the central building. The arc lights were still on, creating an eerie gray-yellow sheen on the concrete block. We came around to the side door and Drill took out a wire cutter, slicing through the wire glass in four deft cuts of the wheel and then pushing through so softly with the tapper, the pane fell to the floor with a quiet, easy thump. Where had he learned that? I wondered. Housebreaking in the Bronx was reaching new levels of professionalism.

Five-forty-seven. We proceeded past some dormitory rooms along a corridor leading to the administrative offices that were at the end, separated by a pair of swinging doors. We continued through them slowly. No one was about. We walked inside, checking the empty desks, personal computers, bulletin boards. A large Mercator projection showed the ''outreach'' of Cosmic Aid, double red arrows for special attention pointing at Thailand, Guatemala, Ethiopia, and the Sudan. There was a list of something called Funding Affiliates and some framed letters from various foreign politicians and dignitaries. The back room had autographed photos of rock and movie stars, most of them posed with Sandollar, and a set of Milanese-type black leather furniture with a sign pointing to it saying DON'T WORRY—IT'S DONATED.

A fire door led out to another corridor, which had the words SUPPLY AREA—HOLDING & TRANSIT painted directly on the wall with an arrow. We started along it, going through another fire door which took us out onto a steel catwalk overlooking a large, hangarlike internal loading bay. But even before we started across it, an alarm began wailing and the lights switched on.

"Shit," I said. "Separate!"

I grabbed Chantal and ran along the catwalk as King and Drill headed down a spiral stairway. Omar and Lancaster started back in the direction we had come, but there was an immediate burst of machine gunfire and they staggered back gasping in our direction, hit in the chest and side. Just as suddenly three of the paramilitaries appeared at the bottom, racing across the concrete floor toward King and Drill, firing at them. I grabbed Chantal, pulling her down on the steel catwalk, when Drill, with the grace of an antelope, leaped from the spiral stairs onto the canvas roof of a military-style transport truck and, without losing his footing for a second, started firing at them with a .45, hitting two immediately and driving the third back where he came from. He then jumped down to the concrete, grabbed a machine gun from one of the wounded paramilitaries, and joined me in a crossfire aimed at the catwalk door, hitting the first two who came through. He then ran up the spiral stairway again, gestured for me to follow him, and the two of us ran down the corridor, pursuing the remaining paramilitaries, including their leader, into a cul-de-sac. While Drill slammed him in the gut with the barrel of the machine gun, I grabbed his AK-47 and rammed his head into a wall, sending him crumpling to the floor. I then turned to Drill, who had already disarmed the last of the paramilitaries and was cooly flicking the shells out of his pistol cartridge. Where had this man come from? Inside of thirty seconds, almost single-handedly and without killing anybody, he had immobilized a small army of vicious counterterrorist thugs right out of the back pages of *Soldier of Fortune* magazine. I had the feeling that if I hadn't been there, it might've taken him as much as a minute.

"Nice work," I said. "I must admit, King King has a talent for picking his allies."

"A talent? I am sorry," he said in a liltingly formal accent. "Until yesterday I do not know Mr. King."

I stared at him, puzzled, when I noticed the New Yorker, pulling himself up on a steel railing behind him while reaching into his right combat boot. He spun around, pointing a Beretta directly at Drill's back. Before I could raise my weapon, a shot rang out. The New Yorker went flying backward, his head snapping and his arms flailing and jerking in the air while his gun skittered across the floor.

I turned to see Chantal frozen behind us with her knees slightly bent and her legs spread apart. Her left hand was unable to stop her right from trembling as she clenched her teeth and grasped her wrist, still training her new Smith & Wesson Detective Special Model 36 on the bloody New Yorker. Her face registered a combination of fear, shock, and nausea as he groaned on the floor.

I walked over. "You didn't have a choice."

She nodded.

"Now you know how it feels."

"Yes. Now I do." She looked down at her hand, staring at the gun as if it were an alien creature like a sea slug.

"And now you had better find that money," said King King, coming up behind me. "And the proof to free my brother." He stared at me coldly. Outside I could hear people banging on the fire door.

I looked down the spiral stairs toward the area where the last of the paramilitaries had come from. I could see a couple of shipping crates, another pickup truck, and a door with the words MEDICAL SUPPLIES—RESTRICTED AREA printed on it in large highway yellow letters against an olive field. "Down there," I said. King gave me another cold stare before we left Omar and Lancaster behind, and King, Drill, Chantal, and I descended onto the concrete floor again. I glanced through the flap of the transport truck—it was empty—and signaled for them to follow me to the door. I expected it to be locked, but it was open and we slipped through carefully, walking down into a dimly lit corridor that looked as if it had been tunneled like a mine shaft straight into the side of the hill. The sound of our footsteps bounced off the concrete floor, ricocheting off the narrow walls, and I hoped we were right when we counted only six paramilitaries. But it seemed useless to turn back now. Down at the end of the corridor I could see another door which had to be the answer to something. We drew closer to it, an eerie organ arrangement of "Imagine," Sandollar's theme, filtering through like background music at a funeral parlor. Suddenly the door swung open and a huge klieg light switched on, glaring straight out and blinding us.

"Well, well, Wine, up early, aren't we? I've been waiting for you. Ever since you visited that scared little redneck in Glendale. Of course, I didn't know you were bringing your own militia."

"Well, Eddy, our intelligence told us you weren't exactly a one-armed bandit yourself. And the way that unemployed contra of yours chased me around New York . . ." I took a step forward.

"Don't go any further," he said sharply. "Any of you. Unless you believe in reincarnation!"

"Hit the deck!" I yelled as I fired straight into the light, diving forward onto the hard concrete with Chantal, King, and Drill like a trio of linebackers. A round of machine gunfire flew over our heads, smashing against the door behind us, but the corridor went dark. Then another light appeared. It was a high-powered Tekna flashlight in the hands of Drill. He was aiming it straight in the face of Sandollar, who stood in the doorway with his wife, Kim, a few feet behind him. Through the door I caught a glimpse of what looked like a staggering amount of cash stacked against a block wall.

"Very heroic but absolutely useless," said Sandollar. "This entire bunker is wired with explosives." He held a small remote control box the size of a cigarette pack up to the light beam. "Before I part with one penny, I'd be delighted to take us all up."

"I imagine you would, Eddy. But then what would happen to Neutron City?"

"Yeah, I'd hate to see that go. But so what? Another rock dream bites the dust. It wouldn't be my first."

"Twenty-five million along with it?" I slowly stood up and took another tentative step forward.

"Charity money," said Eddy dismissively. "Everybody got their rocks off on it already anyway. Got to feel great and generous. Got to go out and rape and pillage like any true child of the eighties without feeling guilty for *one minute*. Now, isn't that a service? Who else is providing that?"

"I don't know, Eddy. Not a lot of people, I don't think. Maybe some evangelists like your father-in-law . . ."

"Him? He's dealing with a different social class. Completely. He doesn't understand what I'm doing, doesn't trust me for a minute, does he, Kim?"

"No, Eddy," she said.

"I mean, what does he know about where we come from, Moses. The idealism and then the disillusionment. And then everybody out for the big score, a society like a big lollipop waiting to be licked. No wonder we all want in. Who wants to be in an old VW van when your buddy's in a Mercedes? Have a Nakamichi tape deck that *really* plays the blues. Every fucking exercise machine in the Sharper Image catalog. What can a Korean evangelist know about *that?* That's not his scene. That's Mars to him. He knows about midwestern gray-haired ladies and lost teen-age Jesus freaks. He doesn't know about *us*. But he had a great scam going and I knew it. And he knew I knew it. Ever since we got married, he's been looking for some way to disown me. But now he's afraid. We know too much about his business. We're franchised. We're a religion, too. They can't touch us. Soon we'll be bigger than he is.''

I made a move forward, but he waved the remote control in my face as a warning and I stopped. By now King, Chantal, and Drill were on their feet too, a few steps behind me.

"Look, Moses," Sandollar continued, "why don't we get smart and all share in this? There's plenty and more to come. You're sick of being a private dick, right? I mean, it may sound crazy, but in the long run we're doing these Africans a favor. Charity can cure cancer, maybe, but it can't cure poverty. All it can do is postpone things, cause human overgrazing, you know, like cattle out in a field that wasn't meant for livestock. That just makes things worse. Or it fosters dependency, like a father who keeps supporting his son until he's forty-five. Who wants that? In the end, they're both fucked. I mean, Wine, you know. Did the Chinese ask for charity? And are *they* starving? I'm teaching the Africans a lesson, increasing their ultimate chances of survival by *not* giving them the money. And the rest of us, we'll be happier listening to the sounds out of Neutron City anyway. Right?''

"Those of use who are still alive.''

"Hey, man. I'm not a *murderer.* I didn't want any of this shit to happen. I just didn't have any choice. If Mike hadn't been so jealous, he could've made a killing too. I would've cut him in. But he went so crazy over me and Emily, he would've spilled everything. And this is the modern world. These things happen. It's just common situational ethics: you don't go and ruin a man's livelihood over a little libidinal excess. I mean, it didn't bother Kim. Did it, baby?'' His wife shook her head. "And Nastase. That Romanian fruitcake I met through my father-in-law. All I wanted was for him to let us in the Picasso suite. I didn't tell him a thing. Or his Glendale Christer buddy, that Billy kid. I didn't know they'd go bonkers the minute you sent that old bloodhound nosing around."

"Burckhardt? What bush did you bury that poor bastard under?"

"Hey, what choice did I have? If I'd had any brains, we'd've offed Billy, too, but I don't have the stomach for this stuff. Not like this guy." He gestured toward King.

"You don't, huh?" I said. "You had enough stomach to have Carl Bannister butchered with a kitchen knife and arrange for Otis to take the fall."

"What? Now that's *really* crazy! What the hell would I do that for?"

"No good reason, white boy. You're absolutely right. You didn't do it," said King calmly. Sandollar turned toward him in amazement at the precise moment King shot him in the face. The remote control dropped to the floor, away from the crumpling Sandollar, and Kim started to scream.

"All right. Enough of this bullshit," said King, suddenly pointing his pistol into *my* side. "Drop it!" I let go of my gun. "You too, bitch!" He slammed the Special out of Chantal's hand, then nodded to Drill, who picked up our weapons and walked out. King gestured for us all—Chantal, Kim, and me—to back up in the small room, behind the money. There was more of it than I had ever seen, even in display windows in Las Vegas, piled in packets of thousand-dollar bills that came up to the waist.

"Gonna retire, King?" I asked.

He laughed softly. Then he looked at us a moment before speaking. "You know, when Otis was a three-year-old kid, our mama went out to turn a trick and left the gas on by accident. Little Otis started choking, but he didn't know what the fuck to do. I mean he didn't know where it was coming from. How could he? At that age. So he keeled over and passed out."

I heard a noise and looked over to see Drill coming down the corridor with a large baggage carrier on rollers. He was followed by the injured Omar and Lancaster. They parked the carrier directly in front of us and started to load the bills. King kept his gun on us and watched them do it for a moment before continuing.

"And by some stretch of luck," he said, "just when he would've died for sure, I was coming back from a basketball game for something to eat—I was eight at the time—and opened the door and nearly passed out myself. But I was smart enough to realize what was happening, so I opened the window, grabbed Otis, and stuck his head out. No big deal, but all his life he thought I was his savior or something. Maybe 'cause his mother was a junkie whore and his father was a jailbird, but even though I might've been the worst dope-dealing motherfucker in the Bronx, to Otis I was more than a brother. I was his God and I was his parents. Even when he came to Hollywood and started to be a famous comic. Every night he'd call me up, tell me how much he needed me, how lonely he was. 'The Tears of a Clown,' like Smokey says. Even that girl friend of his couldn't help him. Only Daddy King and cocaine. Cocaine like a mother and his brother like a father. So when that Malibu shrink made the mistake of using *me* as a guinea pig, of making *my* safety and livelihood *his* way of controlling Otis by threatening to reveal intimate details of *my* business, that shrink didn't know it, but he was a dead man. I couldn't tolerate that. And I couldn't tolerate what he wanted from Otis—contractual servitude for life. He even wanted to be in his will. Can you believe it? And he was gonna get it. I know. 'Cause Bannister was fucking with my brother's mind in the worst way, making him into a slave just when he had a chance, for the first time, to be free. Free of that Malibu Mephistopheles, free of me, free even of that motherfucking white powder. That's why I had him come to New York. So he wouldn't be around when I had Bannister mashed. Hell, I even had 'em use a weapon from the bastard's own house. But even that didn't work out, as it turned out.'' He shook his head. ''You know—it's funny. The only thing that made me really hate who I was and what I did was Otis's loving me so much.'' King stopped and looked over at his men. The money on the carrier was stacking up. ''But that's over now. This is going to be it: *redemption!* I have to make restitution for my life. To my brothers everywhere. And to my own brother. First of all, this is a signed statement of my guilt with everything spelled out in enough detail so there won't be any question. I want you to give this to the police.'' He handed me a sealed envelope. ''Congratulations, Mr. Wine. You just made yourself fifty grand. I understand it's not the first time you've profited well from a corporation.'' He half smiled before continuing. ''You know, that asshole Sandollar was right. Charity's not the answer. Not for anybody. But especially not for black people. It's self-determination. All those starving sonsofbitches in Africa are only gonna get better when they take control for themselves. They don't need a Botha or some other white asshole, Christian, U.N., or otherwise, power-tripping them with their armies and their so-called laws. Even their so-called good deeds. They got their own motherfuckers for that, and when the time comes, they're gonna deal with them, too. But right now they got a war on their hands, a race war, and I want to help them win it. That's why I contacted that dude over there." He gestured toward Drill. "His real name isn't Drill. You'll never know what his real name is. Never! But he works with an organization in Soweto, South Africa, that's going to make good use of this money, every penny of it, in that war. And I'm not talking about charity, motherfucker. I'm talking about freedom! ... *Uhuru!*" he shouted. For all I knew, it was the only African word he understood. And with that, he shoved the barrel of his gun in his mouth and blew his brains out.

22 "A famous comic murdered. Another held and released. His notorious brother a suicide. The dead comic's wife now indicted. And a young so-called philanthropist behind it all. Mr. Wine and Dr. Nathanson, how would you—"

"I've had it!" said Sonya. I was sitting in my living room with her, Chantal, Jacob, and Simon, watching the telecast. "What is this? A road show? We've sat through three of these this week. This is the last time I'm going to listen to

that shrink reduce all criminal behavior to some mother for-
getting to breast-feed her baby at three months! Besides, I
thought you said you'd given up psychotherapy.''

"Come on, Sonya," said Jacob. "They're not discussing
'nature versus nurture.' This is an analysis of the psychological ramifications of one *particular* crime.''

"Psychological ramifications," she snorted. "Proudhon
should turn over in his grave. The root of all crime is economic. How many times have I had to tell you?''

" 'Property is theft.' " Jacob rolled his eyes. "But there's
still something I don't get." He turned toward Chantal and
me. "How come Emily Ptak hired you in the first place?''

"Because," said Chantal, "like most Californians, she had
been seeing a shrink for years. And when all the trouble
started to happen, she was afraid Nathanson knew too much.
So, in order not to create waves, she had no choice but to
go along with his suggestion of hiring a detective.''

"But then she fired my dad when Bannister got it.''

"Panic," said Chantal. "Emily stood to make a fortune
from her boyfriend Sandollar and she didn't know what to
think. And, of course, at that point Nathanson began to suspect her too.''

"Is that right, Dad?" said Simon. "Did Nathanson suspect her?''

But I didn't answer right away. My mind was elsewhere,
back a couple of weeks earlier at my last session with Nathanson. I was sitting in his office, the ochre light of his
Tiffany lamp reflecting off his face.

"Well," I had said. "Now at least you won't have to worry
about getting Bannister's license revoked.''

A large grin spread across the psychiatrist's face. "You understood that, did you?"

"It took a while, I must admit. I played with every possible theory to explain your behavior. And then when you ran off to Koreatown to talk with Reverend Wu"—I shook my head—"I didn't realize you were looking into Bannister's real estate holdings."

"How'd you solve it?"

"Figure and ground." I smiled. "In this case, the figure being the matches from the Bonaventure."

"And the ground?"

"The book it was sitting on." I pointed to the volume of licensing requirements from the Board of Medical Examiners that still sat at the edge of Nathanson's desk. "As you said, it was always in front of my eyes. And considering that Bannister had been one of your pupils, it's not surprising you would go to such effort to see him disenfranchised."

"My *prize* pupil," said Nathanson, for the last time pressing the servo-control that brought him erect in his chair. "Moses, I think you're getting better."

"I'm feeling better. Action *is* therapy."

"Yes, that's all there is in the long run—action." He looked off thoughtfully. "Inside these walls, all I see of the real world is only a guess."

"I'll miss you."

"I'll miss you, too. But who knows? Perhaps circumstances will bring us together."

"Dad, where are you?" Simon was shaking my arm. "Don't you want to see the wrap-up?"

I snapped out of my reverie and looked at the TV. I was on split screen with the moderator, the words "Los Angeles" supered under my face and "Washington, D.C." supered under his.

"One last question on this case, Mr. Wine. As far as you know, is there any truth to the rumor that a large sum of money—millions, in fact—was sequestered somewhere in the bowels of Cosmic Aid in Ojai?"

The camera zoomed in straight for me.

"Not as far as I know," I said.

"Well, there you have it. This is *Larry King Live* for Cable News Network. Good night."

"Thank God you didn't blow that one," said Sonya.

I looked over at Chantal and smiled.

ABOUT THE AUTHOR

Roger L. Simon's first Moses Wine detective novel, *The Big Fix*, won awards from the Mystery Writers of America and the Crime Writers of Great Britain as the best crime novel of the year, and it was later made into a film. *The Straight Man* is his fifth novel.

Roger L. Simon has two sons, Raphael and Jesse, and lives with his wife, Renée, in California. He is also a film maker.